You'd better be good, child—good as gold,

As good as good can be.

Else I'll turn you in to the Vampirates

And wave you out to sea.

Yes you'd better be good, child—good as gold,

Because—look! Can you see?

There's a dark ship in the harbor tonight

And there's room in the hold for thee!

(Plenty of room for thee!)

Well, if pirates are bad,

And vampires are worse,

Then I pray that as long as I be

That though I sing of Vampirates

I never one shall see.

Yea, if pirates are danger

And vampires are death,

I'll extend my prayer for thee—

That thine eyes never see a Vampirate...

...and they never lay a hand on thee.

VAMPIRATES

DEMONS OF THE OCEAN

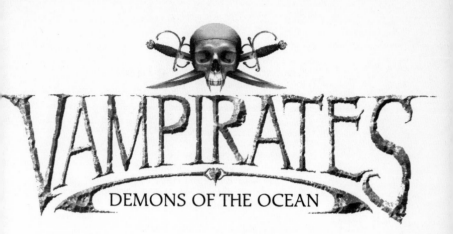

VAMPIRATES

DEMONS OF THE OCEAN

by Justin Somper

LITTLE, BROWN AND COMPANY
New York ∽ Boston

Little, Brown and Company

Hachette Book Group USA
1271 Avenue of the Americas, New York, NY 10020
Visit our Web site at www.lb-kids.com

First U.S. Edition: October 2006
First published in Great Britain by Simon & Schuster UK

Somper, Justin.
    Demons of the ocean / by Justin Somper. — 1st U.S. ed.
        p.   cm. — (Vampirates)
    Summary: When twins Connor and Grace's ship is wrecked in a storm and
Connor is rescued by pirates, he believes that Grace has been taken aboard the
mythical Vampirate's ship, and he is determined to find her.
    ISBN–13: 978-0-316-01373-4 (hardcover)
    ISBN–10: 0-316-01373-0 (hardcover)
    [1. Pirates—Fiction.   2. Vampires—Fiction.   3. Twins—Fiction.]
I. Title.
PZ7.S69733De 2006
[Fic]—dc22

                                                    2006001605
                        10 9 8 7 6 5 4 3 2 1

                        Q-FF

            Printed in the United States of America

            Book design by Alison Impey
The text was set in ITC Charter, and the display type is Exlibris.

For my dad, John Dennis Somper,
with love and thanks for sheltering me from the storm

CRESCENT MOON BAY,
EAST COAST OF AUSTRALIA.
THE YEAR 2505.

THE STORM,
THE SHANTY,
AND THE SHIP

As the first crack of thunder broke over Crescent Moon Bay, Grace Tempest opened her eyes. A flash of sheet lightning broke behind the curtains. Shivering, she threw back the bedclothes and walked over to the bedroom window. It had broken free and was wide open, beating in the gale like a glass wing.

Grace reached out to pull it back. It required some effort and the rain drenched her in the process, but she managed it. She fastened the window but left it just slightly ajar — not wanting to entirely shut out the storm. It had a strange, rough music with too many drumrolls and clashing cymbals. It made her heart race from excitement as well as fear. The rainwater was icy cold on her face and neck and arms. It made her skin tingle.

Across the room, Connor was still asleep — his mouth wide open, one arm flopping over the edge of his bunk. How could he sleep through such a racket? Perhaps her twin brother had clean exhausted himself playing soccer all afternoon.

Beyond the lighthouse window, the bay was empty of ships. This was no night to be out sailing. The lighthouse beam swept across the surface of the ocean, illuminating the troubled waves. Grace smiled, thinking of her dad up above in the lamp room, watching over the harbor, keeping everyone safe.

Another sheet of lightning cracked and splintered outside the window. Stumbling back, Grace careered into Connor's bed. Her brother's face suddenly crinkled and then his eyes opened. He looked up with a combination of confusion and annoyance. She stared down at his bright green eyes. They were the exact same shade as hers — as if an emerald had been cut in two. Their dad's eyes were brown, so Grace had always thought that they must have taken after their mother. Sometimes, in her dreams, a woman appeared at the lighthouse door, smiling and looking down on Grace with the same piercing green eyes.

"Hey, you're all wet!"

Grace realized that she was dripping rainwater onto Connor.

"There's a storm. Come and look!"

She grabbed his arm and pulled him out from under the bedclothes, dragging him toward the window. He stood there, rubbing the sleep out of his eyes, as another vein of lightning danced in front of them.

"Isn't it amazing?" Grace said.

Connor nodded but was silent. Although he had lived all his days in the lighthouse at the edge of the shore, he had never gotten used to the raw power of the ocean — its ability to change from a calm millpond one moment to a raging furnace the next.

"Let's go and see what Dad's up to," he said.

"Good idea." Grace grabbed her dressing gown from the bedroom door and wrapped herself up all snug. Connor pulled on a hooded sweater over his T-shirt. Together they raced out of the bedroom and climbed the spiral staircase up to the lamp room.

As they made their way up, the noise of the storm grew louder. Connor didn't like it one bit, but he wasn't about to share that with Grace. His sister was quite fearless. It was strange. Grace was as thin and bony as a rake, but as tough as an old boot. Connor was physically strong, but Grace had a steely mental strength that he had yet to gain. Perhaps he never would.

"Well, hello there!" said their dad as they emerged into the lamp room. "Storm woke you up, did it?"

"No, *Grace* woke me up," Connor said. "I was in the middle of a really good dream! I was about to score a hat trick."

"I don't understand how anyone can sleep through a storm like this," Grace said. "It's too noisy and too beautiful."

"You're weird," Connor said.

Grace frowned and jutted out her lip. Sometimes, though they were twins, she felt they were polar opposites.

Their dad took a sip of his strange-smelling tea and beckoned to them.

"Grace, why don't you come over here and get a ringside seat for the show. Connor, come and sit by me."

The twins did as he said, squatting down on the floor on either side of him. Instantly, Grace was fascinated, enjoying the chance to watch the raging bay from the highest vantage point. Connor had a flash of vertigo but he felt his father's reassuring hand on his shoulder, sending waves of calm through his body.

Their dad took another sip of his tea. "Who'd like to hear a shanty?" he asked.

"Me!" Connor and Grace answered in unison. They both knew exactly the shanty he would sing. He'd sung it to them for as long as they could remember, from the time when they'd been babies — in matching cots, side by side — and couldn't even understand the words.

"This," he announced grandly — as if he hadn't done so a thousand times before — "this is a shanty sung by people long before the new flood came and made the world so wet. This is a shanty about a ship that sails through the night, through all eternity. A ship that carries a crew of damned souls — the demons of the ocean. A ship that has been sailing since time began and will voyage on until the very end of the world . . ."

Connor trembled with delicious anticipation. Grace smiled from ear to ear. Their dad, the lighthouse keeper, began to sing.

I'll tell you a tale of Vampirates,
A tale as old as true.
Yea, I'll sing you a song of an ancient ship,
And its mighty fearsome crew.
Yea, I'll sing you a song of an ancient ship
That sails the oceans blue . . .
That haunts the oceans blue.

As her dad sang, Grace looked out through the window at the bay below. The storm was still raging but she felt perfectly safe, looking down from such a height.

The Vampirate ship has tattered sails
That flap like wings in flight.
They say that the captain, he wears a veil
So as to curtail your fright
At his death-pale skin
And his lifeless eyes
And his teeth as sharp as night.
Oh, they say that the captain, he wears a veil
And his eyes never see the light.

Connor watched as his dad used his hand to mime a veil.
He shivered at the thought of the captain's horrible face.

You'd better be good, child — good as gold,
As good as good can be.
Else I'll turn you in to the Vampirates
And wave you out to sea.
Yes, you'd better be good, child — good as gold,
Because — look! Can you see?
There's a dark ship in the harbor tonight

And there's room in the hold for thee!

(Plenty of room for thee!)

Both twins looked out to the harbor, half expecting to see a dark ship waiting for them there. Waiting to take them away from their dad and their home. But the bay was empty.

Well, if pirates are bad,

And vampires are worse,

Then I pray that as long as I be

That though I sing of Vampirates

I never one shall see.

Yea, if pirates are danger,

And vampires are death,

I'll extend my prayer for thee —

That thine eyes never see a Vampirate . . .

The lighthouse keeper reached out his hands to touch both children lightly on the shoulder.

. . . and they never lay a hand on thee.

Connor and Grace had known what was coming but still they jumped, before bursting into giggles. Their dad enfolded them in a hug.

"Who's ready for bed now?" he asked.

"I am," Connor said.

Grace could have watched the storm all night, but she couldn't prevent a long yawn from escaping.

"I'll come down and tuck you in," their dad said.

"Shouldn't you stay here and watch the bay?" Grace asked.

Her dad smiled. "It won't take a moment. The lamp is on. Besides, Gracie, the bay is as empty as the grave tonight. There isn't one single ship out there. Not even the Vampirate ship."

He winked at the twins, set down his mug of tea, and followed them downstairs. He tucked them both back into their beds and kissed first Grace then Connor good night.

After he turned out the bedroom light, Grace lay there, tired but too exhilarated to sleep. She looked over at Connor, who once again was sprawled right across his bed, perhaps already back in the throes of his earlier dream.

Grace couldn't resist one last glance at the bay. Once more, she pushed back the covers and padded across the floor to the window. The storm had softened just a little and, as the lighthouse beam swept across the waters, she saw the waves had lost some of their turbulence.

And then she saw the ship.

It hadn't been there before, but there was no mistaking it now. One solitary ship, out in the middle of the bay. It hovered there, as if quite unaffected by the storm around it. As if it was sailing on the calmest of waters. Grace's eyes traced the outline of the dark silhouette. It made her think of the ancient ship in her dad's shanty. The ship of demons. She trembled at the very thought, imagining the veiled captain staring back at her through the dark night. But truly, the way this ship just floated there — as if suspended from the moon by an invisible string — made it appear to be watching, waiting. For something . . . or someone.

Up above, in the lamp room, the lighthouse keeper saw the same ship out in the troubled waters. As he recognized its familiar shape, he couldn't help but smile. He took another sip of his tea. Then he lifted his hand and waved.

7 YEARS LATER

1

THE FUNERAL

The whole of Crescent Moon Bay turned out for the lighthouse keeper's funeral. That day, not a single black garment was left to buy at the Crescent Moon Clothing Emporium. Not one flower remained at the Happy Stem Florist. Each and every bloom had been fashioned into wreaths and floral tributes. The largest of these was a tower of white and red gardenias in the shape of a lighthouse, surrounded by a swirling sea of eucalyptus.

Dexter Tempest had been a good man. As lighthouse keeper, he had played an important part in the safekeeping of the bay. Many of those now standing around his grave, their bowed necks burning in the late afternoon sun, owed their life to Dexter's keen eyes and even sharper sense of duty. Others had Dexter to thank for the safe passage of one or more family members or close friends, rescued from the dangerous waters beyond the harbor — waters teeming with sharks and pirates . . . and worse.

Crescent Moon Bay was the smallest of towns and each of its inhabitants seemed bound to the others as tightly as stitches in a piece of knitting. Such a tight weave didn't necessarily make for comfortable living. Gossip flowed faster through the bay than the rapids up at Crescent Moon Creek. Right now, for example, there was just one topic of gossip — what was to become of the Tempest twins? There they stood, in front of their father's grave. Fourteen years old. Not quite kids, not yet adults — the girl tall and lanky with a rare intelligence, the boy already blessed with the body of an athlete. But truly, they had few blessings to count, now they were orphans and — but for each other — all alone in the world.

No one in the bay had ever glimpsed the twins' mother — Dexter's wife. Some doubted even that a marriage had taken place. All they knew was that one day, Dexter Tempest left Crescent Moon Bay with a madcap notion to see something of the world. And, one day — a year or so later — he returned with a heavy heart and two swaddled parcels containing his twin children, Grace and Connor.

Polly Pagett, matron at the Crescent Moon Bay Orphanage, squinted in the bright light to better observe the boy and girl. She appeared to be measuring them, much like an artist making a sketch. Polly was preoccupied by the dilemma of which bunks to allocate to her new arrivals. True, no arrangements had yet been discussed, but surely there was no option other than the orphanage for these two children. The boy looked exceedingly strong. He could be set to work in the harbor. And the girl, though slighter in frame, was as sharp as a tack. No doubt she'd excel at helping to stretch the orphanage's ever-dwindling budget. In spite of herself, a smile crept across Polly Pagett's tight, papery lips.

Lachlan Busby, the bank manager, turned his head from the fine floral tribute commissioned by his wife (and surely unsurpassed in the churchyard) to better observe Grace and Connor. How poorly their father had provided for them. If only he had glanced across his bank accounts once in a while instead of devoting so much attention to the ships in the harbor. There was such a thing as giving *too* much. This was not a mistake Lachlan Busby ever intended to make.

Busby had his own plans for the twins. Tomorrow, he would break the news to Grace and Connor — calmly and gently, of course — that they had nothing in this world. That Dexter's possessions — his boat, even the lighthouse itself — no longer belonged to them. Their father had left them nothing.

He glanced for a moment at his wife, who stood by his

side. Dear, sweet Loretta! He could see she found it impossible to take her eyes off the twins. It had been a cruel blow to them that they had never been able to have children. But now it seemed that things might have a way of working out. He squeezed her hand.

Grace and Connor knew they were being looked at. It was nothing new. All their lives, they'd been the subject of gossip. They had never escaped the drama of their arrival in Crescent Moon Bay. And, as they'd grown, the emerald-eyed twins had continued to be the subject of rumor and speculation. There is envy in a small town like Crescent Moon Bay, and people were envious of the curious twins who seemed talented in ways their kids were not.

People found it hard to figure out why the lighthouse keeper's son was so much better at sports than the rest. Whether it was soccer, basketball, or cricket, he seemed to run faster and strike harder, even when he neglected to show at team practice for weeks at a time. And the girl provoked equal suspicion — among her teachers as well as her classmates — with her unusual wide-ranging knowledge and strange notions about things far beyond her age and station in life.

Dexter Tempest, so the rumors went, had been a strange father to the pair, filling their heads with curious tales. Others went further still, suggesting that he had returned home to Crescent Moon Bay with a broken mind, as well as a broken heart.

Grace and Connor stood a little apart from the good folks of Crescent Moon Bay. And now, as the congregation at large sang a stirring hymn about the lighthouse keeper's final journey to "a harbor fresh and new," you might have noticed the smallest note of discord in the hot, stagnant air. While Grace and Connor seemed to sing along with the others, the song they sang was a different one, something rather more like a sea shanty than a hymn . . .

I'll tell you a tale of Vampirates,
A tale as old as true.
Yea, I'll sing you a song of an ancient ship,
And its mighty fearsome crew.

2

THE UNINVITED GUEST

It was the day after the funeral and the twins had climbed to the lamp room at the top of the lighthouse. Beneath them, the bay glittered in the noonday sun. Small crafts shuffled in and out of the harbor. From this height, they seemed like white feathers skimming the blue waters.

Connor and Grace had always liked this room, as had their father. It was a place to come and think, to gain perspective on Crescent Moon Bay and see it for what it was — a tiny patch of land, crammed with too many houses, teetering on the cliffs. In the days since their father's death, the lamp room had taken on extra meaning for the twins. Dexter Tempest had spent so much time in the room that it was impossible for either of the twins to enter it without feeling close to him.

Even now, Grace could see her father sitting in front of the window, his eyes fixed on the harbor below, humming an old sea shanty. She found herself singing it, too.

There would be a flask of hot tea at his side and, almost certainly, one of his dusty old books of poetry. As she'd come in, he'd turn and smile at her.

"I say, I say, anyone at home?"

The distinctive accent of Lachlan Busby signaled an unwelcome trespasser in the room. Connor and Grace turned from the window as the red-faced bank manager appeared at the top of the stairway.

"Well, I declare, I'm obviously not as fit as I'd like to believe! Did your father really climb up and down these stairs every day?"

Connor was silent. He had no wish to get into conversation with Lachlan Busby. Grace simply nodded politely and waited for the bank manager to catch his breath.

"Would you care for some water, Mr. Busby?" she asked at last. She poured a glass and passed it into the bank manager's clammy hands.

"Thank you, most welcome, most welcome," he said. "Did I hear you singing something just now? A strange tune. I didn't quite catch the words. I'd love to hear it if you felt like singing it again."

Connor shook his head and Grace decided it was best to proceed with caution. Clearly, Lachlan Busby was not a man who would climb 312 steps purely for a social visit.

"It's an old sea shanty our father used to sing to us," she explained politely.

"A shanty, eh?"

"He used to sing us to sleep with it when we were small."

"A lullaby, then, a pretty song of calming things?"

Grace laughed lightly. "Not exactly. In fact, it's about pain and death and horrible things."

The bank manager appeared alarmed.

"The point is, Mr. Busby, to remind you that however bad your life appears, things could be far, far worse."

"Ahh, I think I understand, Miss Tempest. And, well, may I say how impressed I am at your . . . stoicism, in the current situation."

Grace attempted a smile, though it came out as more of a grimace. Connor looked at Lachlan Busby with undisguised hatred. He was also trying to remember what stoicism meant.

"You two have experienced a loss that no child, no person of your age, should have to deal with," Lachlan Busby continued. "And now you find yourselves with no parent and no income and no home!"

"We have a home," Connor said, breaking his silence. "You are standing in it."

"My dear boy," Lachlan Busby said, reaching out a fatherly hand to squeeze Connor's shoulder, then thinking better of it, "if only this *were* still your home. But, without wishing to pile misfortune upon misfortune, it's my sorrowful duty to tell you that your father died with many debts. This lighthouse is now the property of the Crescent Moon Bay Cooperative Bank."

Grace frowned. She had suspected as much, but somehow hearing the words made her fear more tangible.

"Then we'll live on our boat," Connor said.

"Also now the property of the bank, I'm afraid," said Lachlan Busby, his eyes sadly downcast.

"*Your* bank," said Grace.

"Indeed." Lachlan Busby nodded.

"What more have you to tell us, Mr. Busby?" Grace decided it was best to hear the worst and be done with it.

Lachlan Busby smiled, his perfect white teeth glinting in the sunlight. "I'm not here to tell you anything, my dears, just to make you an offer. It is true that, as of this moment, you have nothing and no one in this world. But *I* have many things. I have a beautiful home, a thriving business, and the most super wife a man could wish for. And yet, the tragedy of our lives is that we have never been blessed with —"

"Children," interrupted Grace. Everything suddenly became horribly clear. "You have no children and we, we have no parents."

"If you came to live with us, you would enjoy every advantage that being a Busby in this town can afford."

"I'd rather die," Connor said, his eyes blazing.

Lachlan Busby turned to Grace. "You seem more rational than your brother, my dear," he said. "Tell me what *you* think of my little proposal."

Grace made herself smile, even though she felt sick inside. "It is very, very kind of you, Mr. Busby." The bile rose up in her throat and she struggled to swallow it back down. "But my brother and I do not need new parents. It's very generous of you to offer us your home, it really is, but we'll do just fine on our own."

Lachlan Busby stopped smiling.

"You will *not* do just fine. You are merely children. You cannot live here by yourselves. In fact, you cannot live here at all. At the end of the week the new lighthouse keeper will arrive and you will have to pack your bags and leave."

Lachlan Busby stood up to go. He turned to Grace one final time before departing.

"You are a clever girl," he said. "Don't be too quick to dismiss this offer. Others would give their eyeteeth for it."

As their unwanted guest disappeared down the stairs, Grace put her arm around her brother's neck and buried her face in the dip of his shoulder.

"What are we going to do?" she said.

"You'll think of something. You always do."

"I'm running out of ideas."

"Doesn't matter *what* we do," Connor said, "just as long as we're together."

Grace nodded. She started to sing softly . . .

You'd better be good, child — good as gold,

As good as good can be.

Else I'll turn you in to the Vampirates

And wave you out to sea.

Connor remembered his father with his arms around them, gazing out to sea. Though the words were threatening, sending shivers down his spine, there had been something appealing about the idea of sailing off into the night. Now more than ever.

He cuddled up close to Grace and they set their eyes on the sparkling waters of Crescent Moon Bay. As bad as everything seemed, they would be okay. Things couldn't get worse than this.

3

THINGS GET WORSE

Crescent Moon Bay was a poor town, but if you could sell a whisper, it would have been the financial center of the world. And that day, in the harbor market, the whispers had just one theme — the offer Lachlan Busby had made to the twins and how Connor and Grace had sent him away empty-handed.

This latest event only confirmed the popular belief in the twins' terrible pride and aloofness. No one in the bay could offer the twins a better second chance than the Busbys.

Strange as it may seem, there was not a jot of sympathy for the strange pair, who had always been misfits but now seemed to have withdrawn utterly into the lighthouse that would soon cease to be their home.

There was just one person, besides the Busbys, who still entertained the thought of offering shelter to the Tempest twins. Even now, she was turning dirty sheets inside out to make up two bunks for them, and emptying out a warped little cupboard to house their possessions. As she added a drop of oil to the squeaking hinge, Polly Pagett smiled. In twenty-four hours, the twins would step through the tall green gates and enter her domain. They had left themselves with no other option.

—◦—

Up in the lamp room, Grace and Connor looked down on the antlike swarm of people below.

"Time's running out," Grace said.

Connor said nothing.

"What are we going to do? Tomorrow night, the bank forecloses on Dad's loan and takes the lighthouse."

Connor wasn't sure what "forecloses" meant but he understood the gist. In twenty-four hours or so, he and Grace would be out on the streets, or bedding down at the Crescent Moon Bay Orphanage. Neither was an enticing prospect.

"Maybe we should reconsider," Grace said at last.

Connor turned his face to hers and broke his silence.

"Can you imagine what our lives would be like with the Busbys? They don't want children, they want *pets*!"

Grace nodded. She shivered. She and Connor had always been free to do what they wanted, go where they wanted, think what they wanted. Their father had given them those gifts. It was a rich and rare legacy and one they could not betray. To go and live in the luxurious and suffocating realms of the Busbys would have been a complete betrayal of everything their father had stood for, everything he had believed in.

"Why can't we just stay here and operate the lamp, like Dad did?" Connor said, unable to see beyond his frustration.

"You heard Mr. Busby. He said he'd already taken on a new lighthouse keeper." Grace sensed that their options were diminishing. "Besides, he'd probably say it was an unsuitable job for two kids."

"Kids!" Connor spat the word out.

"I know," said Grace, "I know. He makes out he's so caring, but you either fall in with his plans, or forget it."

⌐━━◟

The next day, Grace was making breakfast when she heard a plump white envelope slip through the mailbox. Setting the coffeepot to one side, she picked up the envelope, which was addressed in scratchy ink.

Miss Grace Tempest and Connor Tempest, Esq.

Grace opened the envelope and unfolded the thick single sheet of notepaper. Seeing the name at the end, she frowned, then began scanning the words.

My dear Grace and Connor,
Today marks the last day of your old life.
At midnight tonight, the new lighthouse
keeper will be given the keys to the
lighthouse and take on the burden of
lighting the lamp and watching the harbor
below. There is, as my old father used to
say, a kernel of goodness in the nut of
misfortune - you just have to bite down
hard enough to find it. For you, my dear
children, it will not be so hard to see
what good is coming your way. Tomorrow
marks the FIRST day of your new lives.
You will be free from the burden your
father shouldered all these years. Come
down from the lighthouse. Come and accept
a new carefree life such as children of your
age should enjoy. Some say I am a proud
man, but I am not too proud to offer you
a place in my family ONE LAST TIME.
    What do you say? When you think about
it, what other options do you have? My
wife and I will give you everything you

could want from this life. Just ask and it shall be yours. Meet me at the lighthouse door at midnight. Pack only a bag of memories — for we will soon be making new memories, as a *proper* FAMILY!

With open arms,
Lachlan Busby, aka "Dad"!

Grace dropped the letter to the floor in horror and stood there feeling the tide of fear at last rise up over her.

"What's that?" Connor asked, striding into the room, bouncing a basketball. Seeing his sister's expression, he let the ball drop, each bounce a sad echo of the last, until it rolled to a stop in the corner of the room.

He picked up the letter and read it, taking in each sugarcoated threat. Finally, he took the sheet of paper and tore it, scattering rough pieces over the floor like confetti.

"That's a fine gesture, Con, but it doesn't change anything," Grace said. "We've run out of options and now we've run out of time."

Connor looked his sister squarely in the eye, and rested his hands on her shoulders. He smiled and shook his head. "On the contrary, Gracie. *You* may have run out of ideas. But *I've* worked everything out. Now, let's have some toast and peanut butter and I'll tell you exactly what we're going to do!"

4

HELL OR HIGH WATER

Barely an hour later, the twins stood at the gates of the Crescent Moon Bay Orphanage. Each had packed only a single bag of belongings.

Polly Pagett caught sight of them from the office window. She gave a small wave through the cracked glass and beckoned them through the gates.

The twins waved back, but they did not step forward, and a moment later they were gone. Confused, the little woman pushed open the warped door and stumbled out into the bright sunshine.

As she reached the gates, squinting in the bright light, she saw Connor and Grace heading off toward the harbor road and the sea beyond.

"Come back, come back!" she cried. "This is your home!"

"As if!" Connor threw back over his shoulder.

"Good call," Grace said, squeezing her brother's hand.

— — —

In the morning sun, the Busby residence glittered like a fairy tale castle.

"That will be my wing," Connor said, pointing into the distance.

"And that will be mine," Grace said.

"I'll persuade Mr. Busby to let me drive all his sports cars."

"And I'll fill the swimming pool with roses, just because I can."

They both laughed, and for a moment they didn't see Loretta Busby, waltzing through her Tudor knot garden, pruning shears in hand.

But *she* had spotted *them*.

"You came!" she cried. "You came early!" Dropping her shears on the lawn, she ran toward them, wobbling like jelly in layers of pink chiffon.

"Time to get out of here!" said Connor. And, grabbing his sister's hand, he ran.

— — —

The twins only stopped running when they reached the harbor. It was buzzing with activity, as always on a fine morning like this. The fishermen had already returned with their catches. On the wharf, the sorting process had begun. They threw fish into the air like jugglers, this way a tuna, that way a snapper, over here a cod. Beyond the sorting deck, the wharf was crowded with lobster pots, fresh from the ocean. Inside the cages, the purple creatures still moved about, as if looking for a way to escape.

"Okay," Connor said. "We've said our good-byes. There's not much time."

Grace took one last look around, then nodded.

Beyond the fishermen's wharf, the harbor gave way to the moorings of private boats. In the distance, the palatial cruiser belonging to Lachlan Busby gleamed in the sun. It dwarfed its neighbors. Dexter Tempest's boat was moored among the smaller crafts. It was a simple yacht, fashioned in the old style, aboard which the twins had spent many happy hours with their dad. Grace and Connor hurried along the wooden jetty that led toward it.

"Here she is," Connor said. He reached out a hand and touched the side of the boat, his fingers running across its name — *Louisiana Lady*.

"Do we dare?" he asked.

"Yes, we dare," Grace answered.

At that moment, the sun was blocked by a passing cloud. A surprisingly chilly breeze snaked around Grace's body and she shivered at the sudden drop in temperature.

The twins' presence on the jetty had begun to provoke comment. People were stopping to stare and whisper. What were Grace and Connor doing here? Shouldn't they be packing up their possessions and preparing to vacate the lighthouse? The boat no longer belonged to them, as was clear from a hastily erected wooden sign on board —
PROPERTY OF THE CRESCENT MOON COOPERATIVE BANK.

"We've come to say good-bye to our dad's boat," Grace called.

The crowd made sympathetic noises.

"Can we have a moment to ourselves?" Connor asked, bowing his head.

The people moved away, their whispers now indecipherable hisses. They were soon distracted by the arrival at the harborside of two out-of-breath, clearly distressed middle-aged women.

In one swift, smooth movement, Grace jumped onto the boat while Connor uncoiled the ropes that tied the craft to the dock.

"Stop them!" rasped Polly Pagett.

"Grab them!" cried Loretta Busby.

As Connor leapt on board, Grace looked up at the low clouds scudding overhead and felt the breeze run through her hair. "It's a following wind, force two, maybe three," she said as Connor brushed past her.

"Mainsail up," he said. The sail billowed out, filling with the wind that would propel them away.

"Cast off forward," called Grace, neatly winding the loose rope.

"Cast off aft," called Connor, "and we're away!"

Released from all its moorings, the boat slipped smoothly away from the jetty. As Connor gradually let out the boom, the mainsail swelled gratefully with the extra air and the boat quickly picked up speed.

"Good-bye, Crescent Moon Bay," Connor cried.

Looking back toward the lighthouse, he could have sworn he saw his father up in the lamp room, waving them good-bye. He closed his eyes, opened them again, and the image was gone. He sighed.

"Good-bye, Crescent Moon Bay," Grace echoed. "Oh Connor, what have we done? We need food! We need money. Where are we going?"

"I told you, Gracie, we've got time to work all that out. All that matters is that we get away from here just as quickly as we can. And that we're together."

They set the boat's course to the darker waters beyond the bay. Both twins looked hopefully toward their future.

As the yacht picked up still more speed, Connor noticed the wooden sign that still rested on the prow.

"Property of the Crescent Moon Bay Cooperative Bank? Not anymore!"

He grabbed the sign and threw it, like a Frisbee, far out into the ocean. It sank without a trace.

Back at the harbor, Polly Pagett and Loretta Busby found that shared distress can be a wonderfully powerful bond.

"There, there, Loretta. You wouldn't have wanted those unruly children in your lovely home."

"No, Polly, and they'd have just wrecked your beautiful orphanage. Good riddance to them both! Let the sharks get them."

"No, Loretta, not sharks. Let the pirates at them!"

"Oooh yes," Loretta said. "The pirates! Let the pirates have those ungrateful monsters." She looped her arm through Polly's.

"Why don't you come back to my house for a spot of lunch? We're having sour-and-sweet lobster tails. Lachlan will be home from the bank. He'll be delighted to see you."

Polly beamed from ear to ear. Her day had certainly turned from sour to sweet. And better still was to come.

"Was that a drop of rain?" Loretta asked.

"Why, yes, I believe it was," Polly said. "And look how dark the sky has grown."

"A storm is brewing," Loretta said, "and those poor children, all alone at sea."

Neither woman could contain her laughter as they hurried off to shelter from the rapidly deteriorating weather.

5

JOURNEY'S END

The storm seemed to come out of nowhere. It came at Grace and Connor just when they were at their most vulnerable, out beyond the harbor in the open ocean.

It didn't give them a chance.

The sky changed color so fast, it was as if someone had ripped away a sheet of blue wallpaper to reveal a gaping black hole. The heat from the sun vanished in an instant and the rain came down in hard pellets of water that burned and froze them in the same instant.

The water roiled beneath them, like a bucking bronco trying to throw its rider. The boat clung onto the waves, and Grace and Connor clung onto the boat, their harnesses offering little reassurance. What good was it being tied to a boat when at any moment the sea might slice the boat in two or crush it in its rough, salty fist?

"We shouldn't have done this," Connor cried. "It was a stupid idea."

"No," cried Grace, above the roar of the water. "What choice did we have?"

"We're going to die!"

"We're not dead yet!"

Were those tears rolling down Connor's cheek, or was it the saltwater stinging his eyes? Grace found it impossible to tell. She thought of their father. What would he have done?

"I'll tell you a tale of Vampirates," she sang, bravely, "a tale as old as true."

Connor grasped this crumb of comfort and joined in. The two of them were still singing as the boat spun over and the guardrail snapped in two.

The twins were thrown apart and down, down into the freezing, churning water.

⤛⤜

Filled with a strange calm, Connor watched pieces of the boat sink past him down into the darker water below. A strange catalog of cups and cutlery and books twirled past him. He reached a hand out toward them and watched them dance away. He smiled. Beneath the surface of the water, it was calm, a safe haven from the storm that raged above. It was tempting to stay here, and drift with the other broken pieces of his world. This might be a good way to die.

No, he had to find Grace! He tore himself from his trance and, with every fiber of his body, pushed upward through the water. It was hard and it was painful, and it was all he could do not to let go, open himself to the water and sink back down into the darkness.

But Connor was strong and now he used all his strength to fight the shower of shrapnel hurling toward him as he neared the wreckage of the boat. He burst through the surface, waves lashing him at every turn. Swallowing salty water and retching, he looked desperately around, searching for something buoyant to grab on to. And for his sister.

Connor's savior turned out to be a piece of seating. He gripped tightly to its jagged edges, pulling himself up onto the plank of wood as if it was a surfboard. It was an enormous effort and his hands were bleeding. The churning saltwater added to his pain. But Connor took a gulp of air and realized he had done it. He was alive.

But where was Grace?

The storm was still raging, but quieter now. Connor scanned the bubbling water, looking for his sister's face amid the debris. She wasn't there. Gaining control of the makeshift surfboard, he moved through the water, looking for any sign of her. There was none.

The sea grew calmer but it was becoming harder and harder to see more than a meter or so ahead of him. Connor realized that a mist was settling. It grew thicker, enclosing him in his own personal cloud. No! Now he would never find her. He flapped his hands around him, trying to push the mist away, but all this did was unbalance him. He brought his hands back down to the float and, defeated, let his head fall onto its surface. What was the point? If Grace was gone, there was nothing for him. He might as well slip from the float and dive back down into the water. At least they'd be together then.

∼

Connor lost track of how long he drifted. It seemed an eternity, but it might have been only a few seconds, stretched out of all recognition through despair and fatigue. Now the mist was thinning. Through it, he could see the shadow of a ship. It was faint, but he could not miss the outline. It was like an old galleon. He'd only seen such things in books and a model at the maritime museum. He must be imagining it — hallucinating, as death approached.

But no, it *was* a ship. As the mist began to lift, he could see it quite clearly, turning in the water. Why was it changing direction in the middle of the ocean? Unless it had stopped for some reason. Perhaps it had come to rescue him?

Buoyed by the thought, he used his remaining strength to wave his arms in the air and cry out hoarsely.

"Over here! Over here!"

The ship continued to turn. But it *wasn't* coming for him. He could see no one on board. No one had seen him. The mist had lifted to the level of the deck. As the ship completed its turn, a soft golden light fell upon the ship's figurehead — a young woman. If only she were a real woman instead of a painted sculpture. Her piercing eyes seemed to watch him but, of course, they were nothing more than daubs of paint on wood.

Connor was at a loss for what to do as the ship began to move off into the distance. As it sailed away, he made out sails quite unlike any he had ever seen. They were like wings, glimmering with thin veins of light.

"Hey!" Connor called again. "Help!"

But his voice was weak and the ship was already much too far away. All he could make out was the dark silhouette of its strange tattered sails. They seemed to flap gently as the ship made its way. It seemed as if, rather than sailing through the rough ocean, the ship was merely skimming the surface, unaffected by the strong currents. His mind must have been playing tricks on him.

It just didn't make sense. His body felt dull and heavy and now it seemed that his mind must be losing the fight, too. Grace was gone. The last ship that might have rescued him had sailed away. The only option open to him now was to give up and join his sister in her watery grave.

His reverie was broken by a voice at his side.

"Here, grab my arm. You're safe now."

6

PIRATES

Connor had been so transfixed by the mysterious galleon that he had not even seen the small dinghy steer its way toward him. He was pulled firmly inside, onto the little boat's wooden boards. Now that his gargantuan effort was over, he felt utterly drained.

"Just lie there and breathe as best you can. You're half-drowned, but you'll live."

His rescuer's voice was smooth and precise.

Connor could see a pair of narrow boots and the tight leggings above, but as he tried to raise his head higher to see more, a sudden pain ripped through his neck.

"Lie still, boy. No sudden movements. Your bones have taken a bashing."

It was a young woman's voice.

"Who are you? Where are you taking me?"

In spite of her warning, he pulled himself up to see her better. Piercing brown almond eyes stared back at him. Long black hair was swept back off the woman's face and bound, with leather strings, into a tight ponytail.

"My name is Cheng Li," she said.

Connor's eyes took in Cheng Li's strange clothing. Over a thin dark jersey, she wore a leather jerkin. On one arm was a red and purple band, set with a dark stone. It appeared to be the sole piece of decoration on her otherwise utilitarian uniform. About her waist was a heavy belt, attached to which was a dagger holster.

Connor's eyes widened with realization. "You're a . . . pirate?"

"Ah, so the mind at least is intact. Yes, boy, I'm a pirate." She pointed to the armband she wore, as if to explain. "Deputy Captain to Molucco Wrathe."

"Where are you taking me?"

"To our ship, of course. *The Diablo.*"

Connor lay back and watched her row. Her movements were precise and accomplished. Cheng Li was small, scarcely bigger than Grace, but she was clearly strong.

"Grace!" He was unable to stop himself from speaking her name aloud.

"What's that, boy?"

"My sister!"

"We're here, boy. Save the family history for later."

Connor opened his mouth to protest, but he saw that they had pulled up alongside a large ship. Could it be the ship he had seen before? He looked up, trying to decide whether this was the ship with the winglike sails.

Cheng Li had pulled in the oars and was busy signaling for help.

"Bartholomew, you lazy slob," she called, "get down here and help me!"

Connor let out a weak sigh. For the first time, it dawned on him that he was safe. At least for now. He gave in to his exhaustion and shut his eyes.

The next thing he knew, the dinghy was floating. He felt like he was flying but he realized that the small boat had been winched up onto the deck of a vast ship. Cheng Li leaped out of the dinghy before it was set on the ground and lost no time in firing off commands. Now two pirates — a man and a woman — gently lifted Connor out of the dinghy and carried him in Cheng Li's wake. Their job was not made easy by the gathering crowd of pirates who had come to see what was happening.

"Make room, make room, you morons," cried Cheng Li.

The crowd soon parted at her words.

"Lie him down there."

The pirates laid him down onto what seemed to be a pile of sailcloth and rope. It wasn't the most comfortable of beds, but Connor was grateful enough not to have to tread the icy waters anymore. At last, he could rest.

"Don't close your eyes," Cheng Li snapped at him. "Not yet. Try to stay awake just a little longer."

It was such an effort. He was so tired. But he wanted to obey her. He twisted his head around, looking up again for the tattered sails. But all he could see were people. Pirates. They were crowding around him, watching him with interest. He looked back — taking in their uniforms and their cutlasses.

There was an increasing hubbub from the crowd until Cheng Li raised her arm, the dark jewel on her armband glinting. At once, the noise subsided.

"Show's over, people. Let's get back to work, shall we? The sails have taken a pounding in the storm. De Cloux, you will organize repairs on the forecastle. Lukas, Javier, Antonio — now the worst of the storm is over, you can get on with cleaning out the cannons. I don't *care* if it's getting dark — it needs to be done now!"

Connor glanced around. He really *was* on a pirate ship. He felt a shiver of fear. Was this the end of his ordeal, or the start of a new one? One that he had no strength left for.

As the crowds dispersed to tackle their jobs, only Cheng Li, Bartholomew, and his pirate mate remained. The woman pirate was taller and more obviously athletic than Cheng Li. She wore a bandanna around her choppy red hair.

"Shall I fetch Captain Wrathe, ma'am?" she asked Cheng Li now.

"Yes, Cate, I suppose you'd better."

Cheng Li turned her eyes on Connor. "How are you doing now, boy?"

"I'm all right," he said. But, he realized, he wasn't all right. He would never be all right again.

"You look troubled, boy. What's up?"

"It's my sister," he said. "Grace."

"What of her?"

"She's still out there. In the storm."

"Too late, boy — she's gone."

There were hot tears in his eyes. Everything became a blur.

"Please — you found me. Please go back for her."

"I'm sorry, boy. There was no sign of her."

"But . . ."

"Night is coming fast. There's nothing we can do."

Connor felt like his head was going to explode. From deep within him, he could feel a terrible roar beginning. It came deep from his center, flooding through every vein, stretching out along his arms and legs until every fiber of his being was crying out.

"NO!"

"Calm yourself, boy. Be grateful for your own life. Honor your sister, as she would wish."

Cheng Li's voice was soft but firm. It calmed him somehow, though the words were not what he wanted to hear. But what *did* he want to hear? That she would take the dinghy and scour the icy waters for Grace? He knew, deep down, that it would be a fruitless task. There was just no way she could have survived. He had always been the stronger one, physically. Years of playing sports had given him the vital endurance he'd required to tread water until his rescue. Grace was smarter than him. Grace *had been* smarter than him, he corrected himself. There was no present tense for Grace anymore. She had been smarter than him, but she had not been physically strong. And now that had cost her her life.

"Drowning," Cheng Li said. "Drowning is not such a bad way to die."

"How do *you* know?"

"It's common knowledge among pirates. We live our lives on the water. Once, I myself came close to the brink of death. It was much like going to sleep — a gradual release. Drowning is a gentle way to die. Your sister would not have endured much pain."

Again the words were brutal but he drew some comfort from them. They seemed true to him. He remembered the sensation of falling, his possessions cascading down over him. It hadn't been an altogether unpleasant sensation. He had felt a sense of calm. Perhaps that had been his own death beckoning to him, but somehow he had escaped its clutches.

"There was a ship," he said, suddenly feeling compelled to share with Mistress Li what he had seen. "Another ship, before you rescued me. It sailed out of the mist. An old galleon. Ancient . . ."

His own words unlocked other memories deep inside, but he could not yet make sense of them.

"The ship turned around. It changed direction, in the middle of the ocean. As if it had stopped for some reason. I thought it was going to rescue me. I cried out to it. But nobody heard me. Nobody saw me."

Then a fresh thought occurred to him, exploding in his brain like a firework.

"Maybe it had already made a rescue! Maybe it had rescued Grace! What do you think?"

He turned to Cheng Li. Her dark eyes watched him closely.

"The mist began to rise. I caught sight of the ship's figurehead — a beautiful woman. It was almost as if she was watching. And then, the ship set sail. It had amazing sails. More like wings . . ."

At last, something clicked inside his troubled mind.

"Tattered sails that flap like wings in flight."

He wanted to cry out and punch the air. Once more, he caught Cheng Li's eyes. Once more, they were impossible to read.

"Don't you see?" he said, laughing with joy. "The ship *did* rescue Grace. She didn't drown. She's been rescued by an ancient ship that sails through all eternity. She's been rescued by the Vampirate ship."

He had tired himself and now his heavy eyelids fell shut. Yet, in the darkness of his mind, he could see everything perfectly clearly. There was that ship once more, sailing away in the golden light. Its figurehead was smiling sweetly and the tattered sails beat softly into the gathering night. And standing at the helm, all alone but unafraid, was Grace.

7

LORCAN FUREY

When Grace awoke, the first thing she saw was sky. Dazzling blue above her. Then something strange happened. The piercing blue contracted, then began to stretch and separate out into two blue circles. As her senses began to settle, she realized that she had not been looking at the sky at all, but into a pair of deep blue eyes.

Connor's eyes were green, like hers. These eyes were unfamiliar. They stared at her intently.

As they pulled back further, she saw that they belonged to a boy. He looked older than her and Connor — maybe seventeen or eighteen. He had long black hair with eyebrows to match. Looking down at her, he frowned.

"You're going to get me into trouble," he said.

The words made as little sense to her as everything

else, but she recognized a strong Irish brogue in his voice. He leaned forward and brushed her hair back out of her eyes. He was wearing a Claddagh ring on his finger. She had always wanted one of those rings, with the design of the heart clasped between two hands with a crown above. But this one was just slightly different. The hands clasped not a heart, but a skull.

"Who are you?" she asked, shivering. "Where am I?"

The boy frowned again and shook his head. Wasn't he able to understand her? But he had spoken English to her, hadn't he?

"Who are you?" she asked again. This time she heard how she sounded. "Hooooraaaruuu." Her breath was weak, her mouth and tongue parched.

"Here. Drink."

He took a leather flask from his pocket and dripped water gently over her lips. It felt good, though icy cold. She parted her lips and tried her best to catch the water. It took a moment for her mouth to start functioning properly again. She was so focused on drinking that she scarcely noticed as the boy cupped her head and slipped his bundled-up jacket under her as an impromptu pillow. But when she finished the mouthful of water and let her head fall back, she felt more comfortable than before.

The softness beneath her head and neck contrasted with the hard surface that met the rest of her body. She was lying on a rough wooden floor. Twisting her head slightly, she could see a patch of red-painted floorboard on either side of her. But beyond that, in every direction, her vision was limited by a thick mist.

Her head twisted back to the boy, whose face appeared to be floating in the mist.

"Who are you?" she asked once more.

This time, she could tell he understood.

"The name's Lorcan," he said. "Lorcan Furey."

"Lorcan," she repeated. It wasn't a name she had ever heard before.

"Here, drink some more."

He offered the flask to her lips again and she took another gulp.

"Where am I?"

The boy smiled. "Isn't that obvious, missy? You're at sea."

Although she couldn't see beyond him, as he spoke the words, she felt the ship lurch in the waves and heard the crash of the ocean below.

"How did I get here?"

"Don't you remember?" he said. "There's been a storm."

As he said the word *storm,* her whole body reacted. Suddenly, she was back there in the heart of it, the mast cracking above her, the saltwater drenching her already-soaked body once again.

"Found you floating in the water, like a fish," Lorcan said.

"Yes." Now she realized that he was wet through, too, his hair and shirt slicked tight to his skin. His face was pale, almost as pale as the mist.

"Didn't get to you a moment too soon," Lorcan said. "You were on your way down to meet the mermaids."

"What about Connor? When can I see him?"

Lorcan looked at her sadly. In that terrible moment, she understood.

"You only rescued me."

He nodded.

"Let's go back for him. It's not too late. You remember where you found me? He must be near. You must have seen the boat."

He shook his head. "There was no boat. Just you, flapping about in the waves like a salmon in the Shannon."

Yes. She remembered the feeling of the water. So cold. So numbing. And then the memory ran out, like a dream that ends too soon. She desperately tried to summon up more, to go back. Her head ached from the effort.

"A boat can't disappear," she said. "It just can't."

"In a storm like this, even a ship the size of ours can disappear," Lorcan said. "The ocean can be a wicked brute when he wants."

"But my brother, Connor! We're twins. We're everything to one another. I can't go on without him."

Her heart began to pound. She felt the rhythm build, like a bomb getting ready to explode inside her.

"Twins, you say?"

Lorcan's eyes were intense.

"Midshipman Furey."

Grace heard the other voice, but could not make out through the mist who was speaking. The voice was only a whisper, yet it resounded clearly in her head.

Lorcan turned away from Grace.

"Yes, Captain."

There was a pause and Grace heard two heavy footsteps echo across the ship's boards.

"Midshipman Furey, you must go inside. The mist cannot last much longer."

There were a further two steps.

Lorcan seemed to be in a trance. Maybe the ice-cold water was numbing *his* bones now, too. Perhaps the effort of rescuing her was catching up with him. Like her, his ability to see and speak was clearly lost.

"Is this the girl?"

The other voice. Although it was only a whisper, it was undeniably firm and in charge. It seemed to flow into every corner of her brain.

"Yes, Captain," Lorcan said at last. "She was near drowned. Says she has a twin brother."

"A twin."

"Yes," Grace said. "My twin brother, Connor, is out there, somewhere. Please help me to find him."

"Twins." Again, the whisper slowly took root in her head.

Grace wished she could make out the captain, but the mist was still too thick to see beyond Lorcan.

"Take her inside. The cabin next to mine. Do it quickly. We don't want the others to know about this. Not yet."

"What about Connor?" Grace pleaded.

"Take her to the cabin next to mine." The whisper was as firm as before. As if he hadn't heard her plea. Or was ignoring it.

"And then what?" Lorcan asked.

"Then come to my cabin. There is not much time. It will be dark soon and the Feast will begin."

The Feast? What was he talking about? Were they going to search for Connor? It wasn't at all clear.

"The mist is thinning, Midshipman Furey. We must go inside. There's no time to lose."

As his whisper faded, Grace heard the heavy footsteps echo into the distance. She looked up into Lorcan's blue eyes.

"Please," she said, "please look for my brother. If he's down there. The water's so cold."

Lorcan smiled weakly at her.

"Let's get *you* into the warmth."

"But you will look for him?"

"Let's worry about you for now."

He reached down and lifted her into his arms. As he carried her away through the mist, she felt as if she was flying through the clouds. Or else drowning. She wanted to tear herself away and dive back into the water to search for Connor. But her body was filled with a tiredness such as she had never felt before. And though he was little more than a boy, Lorcan Furey's grip was strong.

8

MOLUCCO WRATHE

Connor stared out into the darkening sky, trying desperately to see the other ship again. The Vampirate ship. The ship that carried Grace.

"It isn't coming back," Cheng Li said.

"How do you know?"

"Because, there *is* no Vampirate ship."

"But —"

"Stop." She raised her hand. "And please don't sing me that shanty *again*. That's all it is — an old shanty. A song your father sang, for reasons I cannot fathom, to send you and your sister to sleep. The idea that such a ship could exist is nothing but preposterous. I'm afraid your sister is gone. It's a terrible blow, I know. But that's the truth. You must face facts, boy."

But there *had* been a ship. He could see it again — inside his head, crystal clear. Turning in the ocean. Again, he saw the eyes of the beautiful figurehead and the glimmering sails that seemed to rise and fall like wings as the ship sailed away.

Connor glanced back over his shoulder and watched Cheng Li dispensing orders to some of the pirates. With her back turned toward him, he could see that as well as the cutlass on her hip, she had two more weapons slung over her back. Though sheathed in twin leather scabbards, he had no doubt that the blades inside were as sharp and lethal as her tongue.

"Make way for the captain." It began as a murmur, but the noise soon began to build.

Cheng Li was adamant that Connor had imagined the ship. He'd only just met her but he could see that once her mind was made up, that was the end of the matter. But maybe there were others on the ship who would believe his story — the captain, for instance.

"Make way for the captain. Make way."

Cheng Li broke off her conversation and strode back to Connor. She looked rather irritated. Connor felt his own heart beating. In fear? In anticipation? For what kind of man must it take to command a mob of pirates?

Suddenly, Connor saw Bartholomew and Cate striding toward him. Following in their wake, staggering slightly, was a man of indeterminate age with long tousled hair and small, circular blue glasses. He wore a long sky blue velvet coat over two silver holsters containing daggers, and his tall leather boots, as pointed as knives, jangled with silver spurs. The captain was laughing and engaged in quick-fire repartee with various pirates. He was firing insults over his shoulder, but with a broad smile that caused his skin to crinkle on either side of his glasses. Leaving waves of laughter behind him, the captain finally swaggered toward him. Connor could see that this man was loved and respected by his crew.

"Here he is, Captain," said Bartholomew, before stepping to one side with Cate.

"Well, well, well," said the captain, lifting his glasses. "What have we here? Been fishing, Mistress Li?"

The captain walked around Connor, without saying anything. Connor marveled at the many colors in his hair. At first, he had thought it was simply different shades of brown, but no, there was gray in there — or rather silver, and then, as the light caught a fresh angle, green, too — like strands of seaweed. Among the distorted rainbow were two — no, three — dreadlocks, bound with seashells. It was an unusual look, but he carried it off with manly ease. For all his finery, and somewhat erratic way of moving, you could tell that the captain had physical strength, not to mention the charisma of a natural leader.

The captain stopped in front of Connor, surveying his wet clothes. A bejeweled hand rubbed his stubbly jaw.

"Hmm, you're fresh from the ocean, by my reckoning, but not a saltwater fish."

He lifted his glasses, and for the first time his gaze bore directly into Connor's face. The captain's eyes were large and flecked with as many shades as his hair. His stare was mesmerizing.

"What's your name, kid?"

"Connor, Connor Tempest."

"Tempest, eh?" He chuckled. "That's very good! Connor Tempest, brought to us in a storm."

He reached out a hand. His fingers were laden with so many glistening sapphires it was a wonder he could lift them. "Molucco Wrathe, captain of this rabble. Welcome to my command, Connor Tempest."

Connor shook his hand. The captain grasped him in a firm handshake.

"Thank you, um . . . Mr. Wrathe."

"That's Captain Wrathe," he said, but with a smile. "Now, tell me, Connor Tempest, how you come to be here."

Connor glanced at Cheng Li. Her face was set in an expression somewhere between boredom and impatience. Her arms were folded tightly and the twin holsters on her back were raised like dark wings, poised for flight.

"Oh, I know Mistress Li brought you aboard. But before that. What were you doing so far out in these treacherous waters?"

"We were caught in the storm. Me and my sister, Grace — we're twins. We came from Crescent Moon Bay . . ."

As Connor talked, he tried to keep Captain Wrathe's gaze, but was distracted by the man's hair. The wind was blowing it about and a long dark lock was now hanging down over one eye.

"You're not much of a storyteller, are you, boy?"

Connor opened his mouth to continue, but as he did so, the lock of hair turned and moved back across Captain Wrathe's forehead. And then Connor realized. It wasn't a lock of hair at all. It was a small snake.

"What's up? Cat got your tongue, kid?"

"I'm sorry, Captain Wrathe, but I think you have a . . . a snake in your hair."

There was no doubt about it. The creature had almost escaped from the tangle of hair and seashells and was easing its way down past the captain's ear.

"Aha," said Captain Wrathe, smiling. "Hello, Scrimshaw, have you come to say hello to Mister Tempest?"

He raised his hand and the snake slipped onto it, curling itself fondly about his wrist, like a living bangle. Connor watched, fascinated, as Captain Wrathe held out his arm in front of him, so that Scrimshaw could come nearer. The snake raised itself to look Connor in the eye. Connor wasn't sure what he was supposed to do in response.

"Say hello to the deputy captain, boy!" Molucco Wrathe

chuckled. "Oh, I'm *only* joking, Mistress Li! Just my joke. We all know *you're* second-in-command."

Connor said nothing. He didn't want to make any sudden movement. This snake was small but it wasn't a breed he recognized. It could be venomous, and its open mouth and outstretched tongue were rather too close for comfort.

Captain Wrathe eventually moved his arm and Connor let out a small sigh of relief as the snake was carried away on it.

"All right, Scrimshaw. You've gawked at Mister Tempest enough, now let's pop you back." Captain Wrathe lifted his hand up to his head and Scrimshaw obediently burrowed back into the unruly thicket of hair.

"Now, where were we, kid? You were telling us about Harvest Moon Gulch?"

"Um, Crescent Moon Bay, Captain. We live there. Well, we did. Our dad was the lighthouse keeper but he died and we lost everything. They were going to put us in the orphanage, or worse. We had to leave. So we put out to sea in our dad's boat. We only meant to sail down the coast, but the weather changed. The storm caught us."

Connor's words came out in a torrent. "The boat capsized. We were thrown into the ocean. The boat was breaking into pieces. I swam as hard as I could to the surface, trying to avoid all the stuff that was falling on me. I couldn't see Grace. I got to the surface. There was a broken bit of seat that I made into a float. I looked for her. I searched in the water and all around me, but I couldn't see her . . . I couldn't see her."

Molucco Wrathe's eyes were wet with tears. He lifted a large lace-edged handkerchief from his pocket to dab them dry.

"What a sad tale, Mister Tempest. What a terribly, terribly sad tale. I'm just glad Mistress Li found you when she did. You'll be a welcome addition to our crew. We need more young ones."

"Thank you, Captain Wrathe, but all I want is to find my sister."

"Your sister?" Molucco Wrathe raised a confused eye at him. "But I thought you said she was lost."

Connor shook his head determinedly. "I saw her being carried onto another ship. At first I thought it was this one . . ."

"Another ship? Another pirate ship? Well, it seems your tale shall have its happy ending after all. We'll find the ship and you shall be reunited with your sister."

Connor shook his head. "It wasn't a pirate ship, sir. It was a different kind of ship."

He could feel Cheng Li's stare burning into him, though he didn't dare look in her direction.

"A different kind of ship," Captain Wrathe echoed. "Whatever do you mean by that?"

"Have you heard of the Vampirates, Captain?"

"The Vam-pi-rates? Can't say that I have, my boy."

"There's this shanty, sir —"

"Captain Wrathe." Cheng Li's voice cut through the air, as sharp and potent as a sword.

Captain Wrathe ignored her.

"Captain Wrathe." She would not be easily deterred.

"Hold your thunder, Mistress Li."

"But Captain Wrathe, the boy is confused."

"I'm sure we're all a little confused, Mistress Li, but I asked the boy a question and I intend to have his answer."

"The Vampirate ship is a dark ship that has been sailing through all eternity," Connor said, realizing that he might not have much time. "It's crewed by demons or, at least, vampires."

"What a tale!" Captain Wrathe said. "And how did you come to this knowledge, my boy?"

"My father," Connor said. "My father sang us the shanty."

"A shanty, eh? I love a good shanty. We all do, don't we, lads?"

The crowd of pirates shouted their approval — men and women, all but Cheng Li, who looked angry and bored. At least, thought Connor, the thrust of her anger now seemed directed at Captain Wrathe rather than him.

"Well, let us hear this shanty," Captain Wrathe said. "Come, Mister Connor Tempest. You sing us your father's song and we'll see what we make of it."

Connor took a deep breath and began to sing.

I'll tell you a tale of Vampirates,

A tale as old as true . . .

As he sang, he watched the captain's face. He seemed to be listening intently. Even his snake, Scrimshaw, leaned forward as if charmed by the singing.

Connor's voice was tired and cracked from the sea water he'd taken in while fighting for his life. He was grateful to reach the final lines.

That thine eyes never see a Vampirate . . .

. . . and they never lay a hand on thee.

As he finished, there were shouts of approval from the crowd and a flurry of clapping. Then silence. Connor looked from Cheng Li to Captain Wrathe. The captain stepped forward and put his hand on Connor's shoulder.

"It's a fine song, my boy. But I fear that's all it is. I've been sailing the oceans since I was a babe in arms and I have never seen nor heard tale of such demons."

Connor shook his head. "I saw the ship."

"You saw it?"

"I think so. It turned in the water. It was an old galleon with sails like wings, flapping —"

"The boy is tired and confused," Cheng Li said, stepping forward to the captain's side.

"No," Connor said. "No, I did see it."

But he could see that, as much as he might want to, Captain Wrathe didn't believe him, either. Now Connor was starting to lose trust in his own memory. Maybe he *had* been delirious and had summoned up the image himself. He didn't know what to think anymore.

"Back to business, everyone," said Captain Wrathe. "Wait — Bartholomew, you stay here."

Obediently, the pirates peeled away. Bartholomew hung back, as requested by Captain Wrathe. And Cheng Li hovered, unasked, behind him.

Captain Wrathe reached out his arm to Connor's shoulder, gripping it in a way that made Connor think of his own dad. He tried to push away the memory, biting down on his lip to prevent tears from falling.

"I have two brothers, Mister Tempest. Two pirate brothers. I don't always like 'em, but I love each of 'em to the very depths of my soul. I can see why you'd cling onto anything to believe your sister — Grace — was safe. But, for your own sake, you must face the truth — however awful a truth it may be."

Captain Wrathe looked deep into Connor's eyes.

"You've come to us on the darkest of your days, Connor Tempest, but we'll steer you back into the sunshine. You just see if we don't."

Connor nodded uncertainly, looking up from Captain

Wrathe's face to the ship's mast. His eyes climbed higher still, up past the crow's nest, until they settled on the skull and crossbones, flapping in the breeze. The sky was an almost perfect indigo now but the moon had risen, sending its cool rays onto the white skull.

9

CABIN FEVER

Grace was awakened by the sound of a bell tolling. Like the captain's whisper, each toll seemed to seep into every chamber and crevice of her brain.

Opening her eyes, she found herself in a four-poster bed. She was propped up amid a sea of fresh white pillows and tucked under the softest sheets she had ever felt. She lay there for a moment, utterly still. The sound of the bell gave way to a strange music — punctuated by a rhythmic, almost tribal drumming.

Her arms were bare and, lifting the sheets, she saw that her old, wet clothes had been removed and she was wearing a pretty cotton nightdress, embroidered in intricate detail. Where had it come from? Who did it belong to?

And who, she wondered with embarrassment, had undressed her?

The music was growing louder. Easing herself up onto her elbows, she glanced around the room. It was lit with candles in glass lanterns, which cast the softest light flickering across the wooden walls and floorboards. As she set her feet on the floor, the ship rocked to one side. It took her a moment or two to get her balance.

She stepped away from the bed, noticing that the wooden posts ended in intricate carvings. The canopy above the bed was heavily embroidered. To one side of the bed was a small, open washroom with a china basin and a jug of water. Everything in the room seemed exotic and luxurious. Perhaps these items had been acquired on the ship's many voyages, thought Grace.

Outside, she heard voices over the persistent music. Grace turned toward the noise. She saw that there was a curtain, evidently covering a porthole. A note had been pinned onto the curtain. She stepped closer to read it.

Grace, please keep this curtain drawn at all times. For your own safety.

Your friend,
Lorcan Furey

His writing was rather old-fashioned but wild. He had used a fountain pen, and ink had splattered over the page. What did he mean by "for your own safety"? Both the words and the apparently hurried fashion in which they had been written made her shiver.

She reached for the curtain. It was very tempting to ignore Lorcan's request. Something the captain had said earlier came back to her. *We don't want the others to know about this.* Who *were* the others? What kind of ship was this?

Just then, she caught a snatch of conversation, right outside the porthole.

"I have such a hunger tonight."

"As do I. I have never needed the Feast so much as this night."

The Feast. The Captain had mentioned that, too. It was clearly an important and eagerly awaited event. The crew sounded extremely hungry. Perhaps they hadn't eaten properly for some time. Maybe the ship had only just stocked up on fresh provisions.

Grace pressed her head closer to the curtain to hear more, but the people who had been speaking must have moved on. She waited for a while, fighting the temptation to draw back the curtain and look out onto the deck. Glancing at the candles in the cabin, she wondered if she might extinguish them, so that there was no light, and then risk drawing back the curtain.

Before she had a chance to act on this impulse, a rough voice — right outside the window — caught her attention.

"Midshipman Furey."

"Lieutenant Sidorio."

She recognized Lorcan's Irish brogue.

"Ready for the Feast, Mister Furey?"

"That I am, Lieutenant."

"Thought I heard you out on deck earlier."

"No, Lieutenant. Out on deck? When would that be?"

"Before the Nightfall Bell."

"*Before* . . . how could I? No one but the captain ventures out into the light."

"I know that. But I could have sworn it was you."

"Maybe you dreamed it," Lorcan said.

"I don't have dreams anymore."

Their voices were drowned out by a rise in the volume of the music. Grace pressed still closer to the curtain, her forehead brushing Lorcan's hastily written note. But now all she could hear was the music. Lorcan and his rather suspicious-sounding companion appeared to have moved on.

She weighed up the conversation she had overheard. Lorcan certainly *had* been outside. Clearly, he and the captain were intent on keeping her presence a secret. But what was the Nightfall Bell and why couldn't anyone but the captain go out into the light? It seemed a strange rule.

She waited by the porthole, hoping to hear something

further. She thought she could hear footsteps, but the sound was muffled and it might just have been the beat of the music. It lasted a while, and then gave way to silence. Utter silence. It seemed as if they had all come inside for the Feast.

Grace turned away from the porthole. Facing her was a little writing desk, with a chair tucked beside it. She walked over to the desk. Its surface was crammed with pens, ink, sharpened pencils, and a stack of notebooks. There was something deliciously inviting about the bound notebooks. She lifted an old fountain pen, but it slipped in her hand and the nib pricked her thumb. A bulb of blood quickly formed on her skin. A drop fell down onto one of the notebooks.

Instinctively, she lifted her thumb to her mouth to suck the wound clean. It was something she'd done countless times before, after a paper cut or pricking her thumb on a thorny rose stem. The blood tasted metallic but not unpleasant.

When she removed her thumb, the narrow wound was clean. But there was nothing she could do to remove the mark from the cover of the notebook. She glanced down at the pen, its nib also now stained deep red, as if she had dipped it in crimson ink. She shivered and looked around for a distraction.

Her eyes lit upon a lacquered chest of drawers, painted with unfamiliar characters, and set upon it, an ornately engraved silver hairbrush and mirror. Inset into both were gems that sparkled like freshly cut diamonds. She picked up the mirror, turning it over to look at her reflection. The frame no longer held a looking glass. It was clearly old and broken. What a shame.

Beside the mirror and hairbrush was a small wooden incense burner. It was lit and sent out a rich, soporific scent of vanilla and jasmine flowers.

She was aware of feeling very tired and retreated to the bed, sinking into the comfort of the mattress. Suddenly, she thought of Connor. What had she been doing, idly exploring this cabin? All her thoughts should have been of her brother and how she was going to find him again.

Maybe he had already been found. But, if so, wouldn't they have brought him to her? The captain had told Lorcan to come to his cabin. She remembered that. What, she wondered, had been decided there? Panic flowed through her veins like icy water.

She had to get out of this cabin. She had to speak to Lorcan and the captain. Had to find out if Connor was on board the ship — and if he was safe.

Berating herself for not having done so earlier, she strode away from the bed toward the door. She reached out her hand and turned the door handle. It was a perfect brass globe, engraved with a map of the world. Her hand slipped off on her first attempt. She tried again. The globe twisted but the door did not give. On her third attempt, she pressed so tightly that her palm came away imprinted with the reversed outlines of the countries of the world. Still the door did not open. It was locked.

Brimming with frustration and anger, feeling increasingly tired and weak, Grace staggered back across the cabin, toward the curtain. She looked again at Lorcan's warning.

. . . please keep this curtain drawn at all times.

Taking a deep breath, she lifted the curtain and pressed her face flush against the icy porthole.

Her heart pounding, she looked out through the glass. She half expected an alarm to sound, or else to find herself staring into the angry eyes of Lorcan or the mysterious captain. But there was no alarm. And there was no one staring back at her. All she saw through the window was the deck. It was deserted. Of course it was. They — whoever *they* were — had come inside for the Feast.

Lucky them. She was hungry herself, but they hadn't thought to bring *her* any food. She was hungry and tired and weak. Her father was gone. And now it looked like her brother might very well be lost to her, too. Feeling utterly dejected, Grace roughly pulled the curtain back across the porthole.

As she turned around, wondering what to do next, she saw a bowl of soup on the bedside table. It hadn't been there before, had it? How could she have missed it?

She cupped her hands around the bowl. It was piping

hot and she quickly pulled her hands away. It could not have been sitting there when she awoke or it would have cooled by now. How *had* it got there? *Where* had it come from? She watched steam spiral from the bowl, puzzled. Her bafflement soon gave way to hunger. Like the rest of the crew, it had been some time since she'd eaten and the soup smelled *so* good.

Beside the bowl was a spoon, wrapped in a cloth napkin. As she unwrapped the napkin, a note fell out and fluttered to the floor. Grace knelt down to retrieve it. It was written in the same spidery writing as before.

Drink this. It will make you feel better. Be patient!

Your friend,
Lorcan Furey

Be patient! Grace frowned. She had ended up on a very strange ship indeed. Where no one but the captain ventured out before nightfall. Where you wished for food and it appeared at your side. Where no one was supposed to know she was here. It was too much to take in.

At least they *had* brought her some food. She lifted the spoon and dipped it deep into the bowl. It tasted like no food she had ever tasted before. Absolutely delicious.

10

THE LIFE OF A PIRATE

"You can take this bunk," Bartholomew told Connor.

It was basic, makeshift even. Just a wooden bed frame with a thin mattress and some space underneath to store a few possessions. Not that Connor had any possessions anymore. He and Grace had left Crescent Moon Bay with only the contents of their backpacks. And the storm had stripped them of those. All he had now were the tattered clothes on his back, such as they were.

"You can't sleep in those wet things, buddy. Here's a shirt — and these trousers should fit okay."

"Thanks." Connor caught the bundle of clothes that Bartholomew threw at him. He peeled off his wet things and hung them from the rafters, slipping into the dry shirt and trousers. Bartholomew was a few inches taller than him, and he had to roll up the hem of the trousers and the cuffs of the shirt. No matter — it was just a relief to be in dry clothes again.

Connor sat down on the bunk. The mattress springs groaned. It was clearly old and worn.

"You'll get used to it after a while," said Bartholomew. "We work hard on this ship. Even the moaning mattress won't stop you from getting a good night's sleep."

"Wait a minute . . . is this *your* bunk?"

Bartholomew shrugged. "Easy come, easy go."

Connor was touched by the man's kindness. He was a stranger to him, and he'd given up his bed.

"I can't take it," he said. "First your clothes, then your bed. Where will you sleep?"

"Don't worry about me. I can sleep on anything."

With that, Bartholomew threw down some sacking onto a spare patch of floorboards. He plumped up his kit bag as if it were a fine pillow. Unbuttoning his shirt, he hung it from one of the rafters. Lying back, in an under-shirt stained with sweat and grime, he stretched out as if he were settling down on the plumpest, most comfortable of beds. He fished a cigarette from behind his ear and lit it, slowly breathing in the smoke.

Connor grimaced.

"Sorry, Connor, would you like one? Reckon I've got enough to make another."

It wasn't that. Connor hated being around smoke. But he could hardly complain after all Bartholomew's generosity.

"No, that's cool. I don't smoke, Bartholomew. But thanks."

"Call me Bart, mate. Bartholomew's too much of a mouthful."

Connor nodded and watched as Bart blew smoke rings into the candlelight. For a time, neither of them spoke. Connor wriggled around, trying to find a more comfortable position on the bunk. Sure enough, the mattress whined and a loose spring dug into his back. Saying nothing, he adjusted his position and stretched out again.

"It's pretty basic here," Bart said, letting out a spiral of smoke, "but everyone pitches in. The captain's kind of old school, a bit irregular, but he treats us like his own family. He's a good guy."

Connor leaned toward Bart to lower his voice. "What about Cheng Li? The captain and Cheng Li don't seem very keen on each other."

Bart smiled. "That's one way of putting it. She's a bit of a thorn in his side and he's . . . well, he's like a bloody great dagger in hers." Bart laughed. "Like I say, Captain Wrathe, he's old school. I'm guessing you don't know much about the pirate world?"

Connor shook his head.

"That's okay, most landies don't. See, in our world,

Molucco Wrathe is something of a legend. The Wrathe family is pirate royalty. Molucco is one of three brothers and they're all pirate captains. Molucco's the oldest. Then there's Barbarro. They have some feud going, haven't spoken in years, so they say. But then there's the younger brother, Porfirio. I've heard Captain Wrathe talk about him many a time. Reckons he'll make the finest captain of them all."

Bart had reached the end of his cigarette. He scrabbled about in the candlelight to find the box of tobacco and began rolling another.

"Now, as I say, the Wrathe brothers belong to the old school of piracy, as do I . . . I guess."

"How old are you?" Connor found himself asking.

"How old do you reckon I am?"

Connor shrugged. "Twenty-nine? Thirty?"

Bart hooted with laughter. "Thanks, buddy, I'm twenty-two! But I guess I've lived a bit. Thirty? Mate, I'll be lucky to see my thirtieth birthday. Some other bloody pirate'll have run a broadsword through me by then, I'm pretty sure about that."

He didn't seem too dismayed by the prospect, thought Connor as he watched Bart light the second cigarette.

"Where I come from — where Captain Wrathe comes from — piracy's all about getting what you want, *when* you want. Life's an adventure, isn't it? At least, it should be. I could never be a landie — shut in an office, trapped in four walls."

Connor's eyes roamed around the tiny cabin they were in.

"Oh yeah, it's pretty boxy in here, but this isn't where I live," Bart said. "I live out there. The ocean's my office, thank you very much. The islands and the reefs are the only walls that hem *me* in. I may work harder than the guy next to me or the guy next to him, to get food in my belly, but I'm a free man in ways they'll never know. And you know what?"

He turned to Connor, fire burning in his eyes. "When that sword comes to get me, I'll be ready, buddy. Because I've lived more in these two and twenty years than most blokes do in a lifetime."

Connor felt the power of his words. His own heart was pounding at Bart's speech. He couldn't yet tell why. Was it fear? Fear of death? Somehow, with everything that had happened, death had lost some of its mystery. Death had claimed his father and might very well have taken, or be poised to take, his sister. All in all, Death was like an uninvited guest who just wouldn't leave Connor Tempest alone. He wasn't sure that he felt fear toward Death now, so much as anger and resentment. He wasn't going down without a fight!

"Tell me about Cheng Li," he said, changing the subject.

"You said that Captain Wrathe is an old-school pirate. How about Cheng Li?"

"Mistress Li is utterly new school. She's fresh out of Pirate Academy. No joke, that's what it's called. She graduated top of her class — with honors. Which makes her just about the most qualified pirate to ever sail the seas. But there's piracy in her blood, too. Her father, Chang Ko Li, was one of the most bloodthirsty pirates to ever hoist the skull and bones. He was known as the best of the best. That's a heck of a lot to live up to."

He held the cigarette up in the candlelight, watching the tip burn down.

"Anyhoo, Mistress Li is here as an apprentice. It's the final part of her training. She's done all the academy stuff and this is to test her out, to see how she fares in real-life situations. It's a bit of a joke, if you ask me. Straight out of school and she's suddenly second-in-command. When other, more experienced blokes, well, it just doesn't seem quite right. Know what I mean?"

"Is it because she's a woman?" Connor asked. "How do the pirates feel about that?"

"Oh no, that's not it — we're not a sexist bunch. Take Cate — Cutlass Cate. She's one of the best, one of the most popular on this ship. In a fight, she's the one you want at your side. What she doesn't know about swords ain't worth knowing."

Bart let out a long, deep yawn.

"I've got nothing against Mistress Li personally. She's actually been pretty straight with me. Sure, she huffs and puffs and tries to keep us in our place. But deep down, she's scared. She's just a scared little girl, I reckon. A school for pirates, well, it's just nonsense. Nothing can prepare you for life at sea. Nothing."

Bart extinguished the last of the cigarette, punched his kit bag back into shape, and closed his eyes. "Good night, buddy. Watch out for the rogue mattress springs! They can do a fellow an injury where he least wants one."

Bart chuckled and soon fell off into a deep sleep. Connor lay awake, his ears ringing with his new roommate's loud snores. He was so tired, he had almost gone beyond sleep. His head was spinning with everything that had happened. It was like a dream — a nightmare. If only he could just wake up.

He glanced around the cabin. This *was* real. He was on a pirate ship, and when he awoke in the morning, he would still be here. And then his new life would begin.

And Grace. Where was she? Had she really been rescued or had he just imagined that?

He had nothing to go on but the memory of that strange ship and the curious sense of calm that had somehow flooded through his body at the sight of its figurehead.

He closed his eyes and instantly an image came to him of his sister sleeping. It was a comforting picture. There she was, in the cabin of the ship that had rescued her, tucked up in her bunk. But it wasn't cramped and basic like this one. Grace was in a proper bed, all nice and comfortable.

Where had the vision come from? Connor neither knew nor cared. It was just the life raft he needed to still his feverish mind and send him drifting smoothly into the warm, soft waters of sleep.

11

SOME KIND OF DANGER

At the sound of the cabin door opening, Grace opened her eyes. How long had she been asleep? she wondered, as Lorcan Furey entered the cabin and closed the door behind him. She wasn't entirely happy that he had just charged in on her.

"I'm sorry," he said, as if reading her mind, "I did knock but only quietly. I didn't want to draw attention to myself."

Her momentary anger passed and turned to embarrassment that he had discovered her half asleep in the flimsy nightgown. She drew the sheets up over herself, simultaneously propping up the pillows behind her so she could sit up.

"Did you enjoy your soup?" Lorcan asked.

Grace glanced at the empty bowl. She had been so hungry and it had tasted so good, she had actually licked the bowl clean. That was something she had never done before.

"It was delicious," she said. "But how did you bring it here without me noticing?"

"Ways and means," Lorcan said breezily, "ways and means. I figured your bones needed warming up after your dip in the ocean."

His blue eyes twinkled at her. He seemed more relaxed than before — the skin around his eyes and across his forehead was now smooth where before it had been creased with anxiety. He was less pale now, too, or maybe he just seemed so in the glow of the candlelight. No, she thought, watching him prowl around the cabin, he definitely seemed livelier than before. The Feast must have done him some good.

"What time is it?" she asked him. "I've lost track and I can't seem to find my watch."

"It's the middle of the night," he said, "the very darkest of the hours." Sometimes when he spoke, it was as if he was intoning an old poem.

"Aren't you tired?" she said. "You must have had a long day."

"Not a bit of it." Lorcan grinned. "I slept until nightfall and I'll catch my sleep when the sun comes up."

Ah, now she understood. He must be on the night shift. Yes, that might explain what she'd overheard him say earlier — about not going out before nightfall. Of course — it would make sense to have a different crew assigned during the night. They were quite quiet, though, Grace thought. She couldn't hear anyone else moving about on deck. But presumably, the bulk of work on deck was accomplished during the daylight hours.

"What's this?" he asked, interrupting her thoughts. He was standing, with his back to her, over by the desk on the other side of the cabin.

"What?"

As he turned toward her, she saw that he held the notebook in his hands. He walked toward her, tapping the mark of blood on the cover.

"Did you do this?"

"Yes." She was embarrassed. "I cut myself."

"Dearie me," he said, "let me have a look."

"Oh, it's nothing," she said. "I picked up the pen, but it slipped and I pricked my thumb."

"Let me see," he said, sitting down on the bed.

Feeling cornered, she lifted her hand from beneath the covers. He took her wrist and gently turned her hand palm-side up so he could see the narrow cut on her thumb. Grace was at once comforted and a little embarrassed by his touch. His hands were surprisingly cold.

Maybe that was why her skin had started to break out in gooseflesh.

"Was there much blood?" he inquired, rather tenderly.

"No," she said, wriggling free. "Just a tiny bit. I'm sorry I spoiled the notebook. I tried to clean it."

Lorcan shook his head. "Don't worry about that, Grace. Don't worry about that at all."

She still felt very self-conscious, sitting there in her nightdress.

"Have you seen my old clothes?" she asked. "I can't seem to find them."

"Why, yes, here they are."

Jumping up, he lifted a pile of clothes from the chair in front of the desk. They looked clean and neatly folded. She was certain — well, as certain as she could be — that they hadn't been there before. But maybe she was confused.

"Why, look, here's your watch, too."

Lorcan placed the pile of clothes on the eiderdown and dangled the watch in front of her, as if about to hypnotize her. His blue eyes glittering like sun on water, he released the watch into her palm. She caught it and looked at its face to check the time. It said half-past seven. That didn't seem right. Hadn't he told her it was the middle of the night?

She lifted the watch to her ear. There was no ticking.

"It's stopped," she said.

"The seawater must have got to its working parts."

She nodded, then remembered that it was a diver's watch, designed to be worn deep under the water. How strange.

"Ah well," he said. "Some would say it's a blessing to be free from the ticking of the clock."

Her father used to say something similar. He had never been known to wear a watch, preferring to set his clock by the sun and the moon, letting the ebb and flow of the light and the tide mark out his day. Maybe that was how it was on this ship, too — with the crew changing over from the day to the night, from the night to the day.

Lorcan smiled at her and glanced about the cabin. Noticing the note pinned to the curtain, he raised his eyes.

"Apologies for the melodrama," he said. "It's just better that no one else knows you're here. Not yet."

"Why is that?" Grace asked.

As he considered his answer, Lorcan's mood seemed to shift again. She saw the familiar furrows crossing his brow.

"'Tis the captain's orders, Grace. He feels it's safer that way."

"Safer? Am I in danger?"

"Danger? No, no — of course not."

"Lorcan, you're not making sense. If it's safer that I'm kept hidden, then I must be in some kind of danger."

He said nothing — but he was frowning.

"If I *was* in some kind of danger, you would tell me, wouldn't you?"

"Yes, of course, Grace."

He looked anxious. His jovial mood now seemed quite vanquished.

"What's wrong?" she asked.

His eyelids shut for a moment. She couldn't help but notice how long his dark eyelashes were. In the lamplight, they cast long shadows over his face.

"This is no ordinary ship," he said, opening his eyes. "Our ways are strange. I'm not sure you're going to like it here."

What on earth did he mean?

"W-why?" she stammered. "Why wouldn't I like it here?"

He shook his head, as if trying to stop dark thoughts from slipping free from their shackles.

"I wish I could tell you more, but the captain has asked me not to."

"Why?"

"He doesn't want to scare you. Oh, I'm making a hash of this . . ."

"Yes. Now you *are* starting to scare me."

"That isn't my intention. Truly, Grace, it's the last thing I want to do."

"Then stop talking in riddles!" she said in exasperation, then felt she might have overstepped the mark.

"Riddles?" he said. "I can see why you would think that, but it's not such a puzzle really."

She sighed. Every one of his answers seemed designed to open up yet more questions.

"You'll be wanting to know about your brother," he said.

She was surprised by his directness on this subject. She had wanted to ask him about Connor ever since he had entered the cabin again, but she had been waiting for the right moment. It was vital, she realized, to gain his trust.

"Do you have news of Connor?" she asked, trying to maintain a neutral voice and not reveal how much she desperately needed to know.

"The captain says your brother is alive and well."

"He says that? How does he know? Is Connor on board this ship?"

"I can't tell you anything more."

"You have to, Lorcan. You said I should be patient and I have been. You've talked in riddles about this ship and why I must be kept cooped up here like an animal, and I haven't pushed you for answers. But when it comes to my brother, I have to know everything. It's too important."

She looked deep into his eyes, feeling something akin to vertigo as she tumbled into the depths of blue.

"All I can tell you is to trust the captain. If the captain says your brother is safe, then you must believe that."

"But how? How can I? How does *he* know?"

"The captain knows many things," Lorcan said, "more

things than I could ever keep in my head if I lived a thousand years."

She didn't understand, but she could see that she had got as much of an answer as he would give . . . for now. She'd have to wait. Gain his trust further. Then he'd tell her more. She'd seen already that Lorcan had a habit of letting slip a little more than he intended. In the meantime, she needed to find out more about the captain. You couldn't trust a disembodied whisper, and that — at this point — was all the captain was to her.

Suddenly, they heard the sound of voices outside.

"Come back here!"

"No, you've had enough . . ."

"Enough? I'LL tell YOU when I've had enough!"

Frowning, Lorcan leaped to the curtain. Both he and Grace listened but heard no more. Until . . .

"No! Let me go!"

"Don't try to fight me. You know you won't win."

Lorcan charged past Grace, toward the door.

"I have to go."

He threw open the door and leaped out into the corridor. The door swung back shut. Grace waited for the sound of the key in the lock but it seemed that Lorcan was in such a hurry he had forgotten to lock her in again. Her heart raced. The scene outside had given her a chance.

Grabbing the pile of clothes, she threw off the embroidered nightdress and quickly put on her old things. She was just knotting the laces on her shoes when she heard voices again, outside her window.

"Leave him, Sidorio. He's weak." It was Lorcan.

"And my hunger is strong."

"You've supped already tonight. You've had your share."

"It isn't enough."

"You know it is. The captain tells us . . ."

"Maybe I'm tired of being told things by the captain. Maybe I'm ready to make my own decisions."

Though unsure exactly what they were talking about, Grace had heard enough to be extremely worried. This time, she wouldn't just listen. She darted around the cabin, blowing out the candles. As the last flame was extinguished, she found herself cloaked in utter darkness. It took her a moment to get her bearings and for her eyes to find their hold in the darkness. But then she stepped up to the curtain and drew it slowly back.

She pressed up to the glass and looked outside. Lorcan's back was toward her. He seemed to be fighting somebody — presumably the man he called Sidorio.

"Go to your cabin," she heard Lorcan cry.

At that, a third figure darted past the window. An old man. A face pale and contorted with fear. Empty eyes.

Lorcan and Sidorio wrestled and Lorcan was pulled around. Suddenly, Grace could see Sidorio's face. He was looking right at her. It was the most horrific sight she had ever seen. The man's features were horribly distorted —

his eyes like pools of fire, his mouth engorged with blood. He looked more like a wild, rabid dog than a man. He seemed not just to be looking at her but into her.

Suddenly, Lorcan turned and saw her looking out of the glass. The shock in his eyes was evident.

At that, the curtain fell from her hand. It didn't feel so much as though she had let it fall — more that it had been tugged free. Regardless, the porthole was closed to her once more. She tried to pull it back, but it felt as heavy as iron. She must be growing weak — or else, some dark magic was at work.

Then, one by one, all the candles she had extinguished flickered back into life. How could this be happening? Grace stood, amazed, as the cabin was filled with light again. She raced toward the door but, as her hand touched the handle, she heard the crunch of the turning lock. She twisted the handle but it was too late. Once again, she was locked inside the cabin. Who was doing this? It couldn't possibly be Lorcan. He couldn't move that fast.

Turning back to the bed, her eyes fell on a cup and saucer, sitting on the table. A spiral of steam rose in the air — as if to underline the fact that the cup had just been delivered to her as suddenly and mysteriously as the bowl of soup.

She approached the cup and saucer, filled with fear and amazement. Giddily, she inhaled the overpowering scent of hot chocolate, infused with orange and nutmeg. It awoke a gnawing hunger deep within her — a hunger she had been unaware of only moments before.

The more she saw of this ship, the more time she spent on board, the less any of it made sense.

"Drink the hot chocolate," said a voice inside her. It belonged to a whisper inside her head. "Drink."

She had heard that voice before. It belonged to the captain.

12

A GENTLE WAY TO DIE

Breakfast on the pirate ship was organized chaos. The mess room, appropriately named, was full to bursting with pirates when Bart led Connor inside.

"Quick, grab those seats, mate. They'll be gone in a jiffy."

Somehow Connor managed to slide through the hordes and plant his butt on a wooden bench, stretching out his hand to save a place for Bart. The men opposite him looked up from their plates.

"Haven't seen *you* before," one of them said. His mouth opened to reveal a desert of space, broken only by a few stumps of rotten brown teeth and scraps of food.

"He must be that kid that Mistress Li fished out of the stew," said the man next to him, leaning forward to get a better look.

Connor nodded, trying to ignore the man's foul breath. "I was shipwrecked. Cheng Li rescued me."

"Did she indeed?" said the first one. "So now what? You gonna be a pirate?" He chewed away on a piece of bread, considerably challenged by his lack of functioning teeth.

"Maybe," Connor said.

"Think you got the guts for it, boy?" the other pirate asked, studying him intently. "Takes a lot of guts to be a pirate."

"A lot of guts, that's right," echoed his toothless neighbor. "And the Stinkbomb here, he knows all about guts. I say he knows all about guts!"

With that, the toothless pirate prodded his mate in the center of his bulging belly. He was unable to hold in his laughter. Great guffaws blasted through his ugly face and he showered Connor with a spray of half-chewed bread crumbs. The other one —"the Stinkbomb"— tittered nasally before letting out three loud farts in quick succession.

Thankfully, at that moment, Bart arrived at the table bearing two plates laden with food. He scooted into the seat next to Connor and plunked the plates down on the table.

"I see you've made the acquaintance of Toothless Jack and the Stinkbomb." Under his breath, Bart added, "Two of the most useless excuses for pirates you'll ever meet."

Connor smiled and looked down at his groaning plate. He wasn't sure what everything was, but it smelled pretty good and he was starving. There were eggs in there somewhere, and some mush that tasted a bit like porridge and was satisfyingly filling. A charred chunk of something — possibly bacon, maybe saltfish — whatever, it tasted good. And a hefty piece of watermelon. It all slipped down like a treat.

"Reckon you needed that, buddy."

"Mmm," Connor said as he licked his lips, "is there any more?"

"You'll be lucky, Oliver Twist," Bart said. "Why do you think I piled the plates so high to begin with? The trick here is when you see food, grab it — and grab as much as you can. The kitchen's well stocked at the moment but that ain't always the case. Now, why don't you go and fetch us a couple of mugs of tea? Milk, no sugar, thanks."

He pushed Connor in the direction of the counter. Connor did the best job he could of weaving through the bustling pirate throng. They were a mixed bunch — young, old, fat, thin, tall, small, and every nationality you could think of. As many women as men . . . and they seemed just as noisy and unruly as their male counterparts.

At last, he could see the hatch that led into the galley. He surged forward, and a young man, with a round face the color of beets, liberally sprinkled with acne, cried, "Yesss?"

"Um, two teas, please."

Almost before the words had left his mouth, two large enamel mugs of steaming tea were thrust into his hands.

"Move it along, sonny," bellowed the pirate behind him, nearly blowing out one of Connor's eardrums.

The room was full of action. As he weaved his way back to the table, Connor passed pirates arm wrestling across empty plates and rolling up the first tobacco of the day, while others got in a quick game of cards before their labors began in earnest.

Toothless Jack and his foul-smelling mate passed Connor on their way out of the mess.

"Have fun, Captain Courageous!" Jack grinned.

Connor frowned and pushed on as the Stinkbomb noisily let rip once more. Connor was mightily glad he was sharing a cabin with Bart.

He had almost reached the table when he felt a hand on his shoulder. Turning, he found himself facing Cheng Li.

His heart began pounding. She was the last person he wanted to see.

"I need to speak to you," she said. "Let's go outside."

Connor looked over at Bart, who stood up and began walking toward them.

"I'll talk to the boy alone," Cheng Li said. "Leave those teas here."

It was a sunny morning but nevertheless a strong wind was blowing around the deck. The sound of the billowing sails, as they passed underneath, was deafening. Some of the pirates were already busy going about their duties — repairing the rigging, cleaning the cannon, climbing the rigging to take their watch. Cheng Li led Connor to a sheltered spot on the foredeck. It was quieter here and they were all alone.

"I wanted to apologize," she said.

Connor could hardly believe his ears. It was the very last thing he had expected to hear.

"Yesterday was a terrible day for you, boy, and I fear that I was not as considerate of your feelings as I might have been."

"Thank you." He couldn't think what else to say.

Cheng Li looked strangely at him. He realized that she was trying to smile. It appeared to be a torturous effort for her facial muscles and eventually she gave up.

"How are you doing today, anyhow?"

"I'm okay," he said. He felt better than okay, actually. Food and sleep had restored his energy levels and he still felt the strange sense of calm that had come out of nowhere and flooded through his body the night before.

"It would seem that even Bartholomew's snores didn't prevent you from sleeping," she said. Although she didn't quite manage a smile, her eyes sparkled just a little.

"Almost," Connor chuckled, "but not quite."

"And so, today, you begin your new life as a pirate."

He nodded.

"Any idea what to expect?"

"Not really." He shook his head, looking around the deck. More of the pirates had come up from breakfast and were joining the others in their chores. It seemed there was a lot to be done and everyone knew their places.

"It's a good time to join up," Cheng Li said to him, "especially for someone like you, who has . . . who needs a change. Piracy is changing, Connor. Our powers grow daily. If you work hard and learn fast, you could find it a very good life. There's a lot I can teach you."

Connor remembered Bart telling him about Cheng Li's training at Pirate Academy. Clearly, she was ambitious and committed. He was flattered that she saw potential in him and couldn't help but feel rather guilty that he had no real interest in being a pirate. But *she* didn't need to hear that, nor did Captain Wrathe, Bart, or any of the others. His one and only goal was to find Grace — to find that ship that none of them believed existed but that he had seen as clearly as he now saw Mistress Li, standing there before him.

"I've been thinking," she said. Her voice was utterly businesslike again. "Last night, I lay awake in my bunk and I reflected upon what you told us."

Again, Connor could hardly believe his ears.

"I thought about that shanty of yours and about how you described seeing the ship just before I rescued you."

"You . . . you believe me?"

"I never doubted that you thought you saw it. I've just been puzzling over whether such a ship could really exist."

"It could," Connor said. "It does."

Cheng Li shook her head. "You have no proof, Connor."

"The shanty . . ."

"That isn't proof. A song won't help you to find your sister."

"Last night," he said, "just before I went to sleep, I had this image of Grace sleeping safely on the ship." He smiled at the memory. The image had been so strong he had almost been able to feel the softness of her pillow.

"Excellent," Cheng Li said. "So, we now have one vision, one dream, and an old song to go on. Really, boy, that's about as much use to me as a paper cutlass. I'm looking for hard facts and you're giving me whims and fantasies."

Connor frowned. Did she believe him or didn't she?

"I'm telling you everything I can," he said.

"It's probably safest to give up on this," she said crushingly. "It's probably best not to get your hopes up. Captain Wrathe would berate me severely if he knew I was even having this conversation . . ."

"I won't tell him," Connor said, desperate not to lose her — albeit shaky — allegiance.

Cheng Li looked out to the horizon. "Could there really be such a ship?"

Connor smiled. He knew that there could be. He could feel it in his veins. The Vampirate ship was out there somewhere and Grace was aboard. It wasn't just a matter of him believing it now. Whatever her bluster, he could tell that Cheng Li believed it — *wanted* to believe it — too. He had an ally.

"Of course," she said, "there's one rather important fact we've overlooked."

Connor turned to her.

"Let's suppose, *just suppose,* for a moment that the Vampirate ship *does* exist. And let's suppose that this ship does have your sister aboard . . ."

"Yes," Connor said, impatient for her to continue.

"There's no easy way to say this, boy. If it's a ship of demons — of *Vampirates* — what do you suppose they want with your sister?"

She might as well have pierced his heart with an icicle. Connor felt her words cut through him but he couldn't disregard the truth of them. What a fool he'd been. Here he'd been clinging on desperately to the idea that Grace had been rescued by the Vampirate ship. But even if she was on board, it wasn't a rescue. And even if she was still alive this very morning, she might not be for long. Cheng Li had said before that drowning was a gentle way to die. Death at the hands of the Vampirates was unlikely to be quite so peaceful.

13

BROKEN MIRROR

"How long have I been here?" Grace asked, as Lorcan stepped into her cabin, bearing a tray of food.

"And a good day to you, too!" he said, smiling.

"How long have I been here? How many days?"

"Let me see," he said, setting the tray down on the desk opposite her bed. "Why, I believe it's been . . . three days and nights. No, no, I'm wrong. Make that four."

Four days and four nights. Grace trembled. If he hadn't told her, she would have had no clue. Since her arrival on the ship, she had found it impossible to keep track of time. Of course it didn't help that her watch had stopped and that there was no clock in the cabin. Being stuck in here, with the curtain drawn, she was mostly deprived of daylight.

She felt tired so much of the time that it added to her sense of disorientation.

"I brought you some hot porridge," he said. "You must be hungry."

She was hungry but she had questions for him and he was becoming far too skillful at deflecting them. He'd lull her into eating the food and then she'd feel tired and lose focus on what she'd been waiting to ask him. And, after a time, she'd close her eyes and drift off to sleep. And when she woke he'd be gone — her questions unanswered. But no — not this time.

"Lorcan, where is my brother?"

"I don't know that, Grace," Lorcan said. "You know I'd tell you if I did."

"It's been four days," she said. "I want to see Connor. I need to know where he is. I need to know he's all right." She was close to tears from a mixture of exhaustion and frustration.

"I'm sorry, Grace. Truly I am. But I have no answers for you. Only the captain can answer those questions."

"Then I must see the captain," she said, suddenly purposeful. "Would you take me to him?"

"I'll have to talk to him first. I can't just take you to his cabin."

"Why not?"

"I'll talk to him, Grace."

"Today? Tonight?" She clasped her head. "Is it day or night? I don't know."

"It's night, Grace," he said, taking her trembling hands and holding them for a moment. "Yes, I'll talk to him tonight," he said softly. "Now, will you not taste some of this porridge while it's still hot?"

"It will stay hot," she said. "It always does. Just like these candles never burn down." She got up and stared into one of the glass lamps. "I've been here four days and these candles are always lit, except the one time when I blew them all out. And then they all lit up again. Explain *that* to me!"

Lorcan smiled and shook his head. "I told you this was no ordinary ship."

"But what kind of ship *is* it?"

Her question hung there. He looked into the space between them as if waiting to pluck just the right words from out of the air.

"'Tis the kind of ship where girls grow tired and weak if they don't eat. Come on, Cook made it especially for you. It would break her heart to see it uneaten, so it would."

"If you want it, *you* eat it," she said.

He shook his head. "I have no hunger."

"All right. All right. If it will make you feel any better, I'll eat your porridge."

She brushed past him and sat down at the desk. There,

on the tray was a large white bowl full of hot porridge. It did smell good. Also on the tray was a jug of cream and a bowl of brown sugar crystals. As usual, the spoon had been wrapped in a starchy white cloth napkin. And, as usual, Grace found the food impossible to resist. She unwrapped the napkin from the spoon and sprinkled sugar over the porridge. She watched as the heat of the oats melted the sugar crystals into a deliciously thick syrup. Then she plunged in her spoon and ate hungrily.

"There now, you'll feel better for that," said Lorcan, who had sat down on the edge of the bed while she ate.

Porridge was supposed to give you energy. She remembered that from home economics class. But, like all the food she ate on board the ship, this left her feeling full but tired. Grace turned away from the desk and faced Lorcan again.

"Are you drugging my food?"

"What?" He laughed.

"You heard me. Every time I eat or drink something, I feel so tired. Then I sleep for hours at an end — or what I *think* is hours. I really have no sense of time."

"Grace, you nearly drowned the other day. When I found you, there was barely a flicker of life in you. The body and mind take time to heal. Has it not occurred to you that maybe you just need to sleep?"

It did make sense when he put it like that. Lorcan Furey had a remarkable knack for calming her dark fears. He seemed able to make sense of everything, but when he left her — when she awoke alone — all that gnawing, pulsating dread crawled back inside her head.

"I'm going to go," he said, standing up. "I shall find the captain and ask him for news of your brother. You're right. You must have news of him. It isn't fair."

He strode to the door.

"Are you sure I couldn't just come with you? Oh, I'd do anything to get out of this cabin for a bit."

He shook his head. "I must go alone. But I understand. Really, I do. I'd hate to be cooped up in here — though it is one of the best cabins on board and," he pointed to the small washroom, "one of the few with en suite facilities. But, like I keep telling you, it's for your own safety. I shan't be long and while I'm gone . . ."

"I know," she said, "I know — don't look out of the window."

"I was going to say — try not to worry. But yes, since you mention it, please keep the curtain drawn."

She nodded. He smiled at her and then slipped out through the door, locking it behind him.

She was tired again. Of course she was. There had to be something in the food. And although she kept blowing out the incense, it seemed to keep relighting itself, sending its heady scent of vanilla and jasmine through the cabin. At first, she had thought the smell delicious — now it was cloying. She felt so sleepy. So very sleepy.

No. She had to stay alert. This was too important. She had to stay alert and await Lorcan's return. She looked around the room once more for something to distract her. Her eyes fell onto the notebook and pens on the desk. Suddenly, she had a flash of inspiration.

She lifted the food tray off the desk and laid it onto the floor. Then she picked up one of the notebooks, smoothed it open, and took up one of the pens.

"Day four," she wrote. "Porridge. Lorcan has gone to ask the captain about Connor. Also asked him about candles and if my food is drugged . . ."

She looked down at the words. It was not exactly poetry, but it might help her to better keep track of time.

Just then, she heard noises on the deck — footsteps and voices. She set down the pen and walked over to the curtain. With the window shut, it was possible to hear voices only if they were right outside or if people shouted. For now, the noise was indistinct. That meant that people were not directly outside and that she could probably chance a look out.

It wasn't the first time she had disobeyed Lorcan's warning — not the second, nor the third. She had grown practiced at pulling back the curtain only a fraction and blocking out the candlelight by pressing her face close to the windowpane.

She did so now, once more, looking from side to side, searching for any sign of the crew. The deck looked empty at first. Then, out of the corner of her eye, she saw a gaggle of people milling about by one of the guardrails. She tried to catch their voices but they were too far away.

"Come closer," she whispered.

As if her words had enchanted them, the people moved away from the guardrail and walked into her field of vision. Grace pressed more tightly to the sliver of glass, desperate to ensure that not one flicker of candlelight showed from inside the cabin.

She watched the people pass by. She heard fragments of sentences but nothing she could piece together. One of the crowd, she realized with a start, was the man who had stared at her that other night when she'd been caught looking out of the window. Sidorio — that was his name. And he hadn't so much as stared *at* her as *through* her. She remembered the way his face had mutated, his eyes like pools of fire. But now he seemed like a normal man. It was as if she had simply imagined the strange metamorphosis. Perhaps she had. Perhaps it had only been a feverish dream.

She heard the lock turning once more. Lorcan. Quickly, she dropped the curtain and jumped back onto the bed.

Lorcan slipped back inside, once more turning the key in the lock.

"I have spoken with the captain," Lorcan said.

"Thank you." Her heart was racing. "What did he say? Is Connor here?"

"He told me to tell you that your brother is safe but he is not on board this ship."

"Not on board? Then how does he know he's safe?"

"The captain knows."

She felt her frustration flooding over her again. "So when *is* the captain coming to talk to me?"

"That can't happen tonight, Grace."

"So you're taking *me* to *him*."

"Now is not the time, Grace. The captain has many other tasks to attend to."

Many other tasks? What could be so important as this? What kind of monster was the captain to ignore her pleas? How could he be so cruel? She was close to tears.

Lorcan turned his back to her, as if he was about to leave the room.

"Don't leave me here alone," she said.

He turned, smiling. "I'm not leaving." He had something in his hands. It was the hand mirror that she'd found on the lacquered chest. The one with no glass.

"Take this," he said.

She looked at him questioningly.

"Trust me. It's a gift from the captain."

A gift? A gift of a broken mirror? She was getting to dislike the captain more and more. Was this his idea of a joke?

"Take it from my hands," Lorcan said.

Grace shrugged. It would do no harm to take it, though a fat lot of good it would be to her. But as she held the ornate mirror in her hands, something strange happened. A trail of mist began to waft around her. It was coming from the mirror itself — from the panel where the looking glass should have been. She looked up at Lorcan, confused, but she could barely see him, the mist was forming so quick and so thickly. Before she knew it, she was standing in the center of a thick white cloud. It made her feel thoroughly dizzy.

And then, the mist cleared. But she was no longer in the cabin. She was on an outside deck. She looked down at the deckboards. They were a natural brown — unlike the red-painted boards she'd seen earlier. She drew her eyes up again and there, standing less than a meter away from her, was Connor.

"Connor," she said, smiling broadly and running toward him. But as she ran, he moved farther away from her. Or rather, he remained the same distance away. She stopped running, realizing that she had not, in fact, moved.

"Connor," she called once more. He did not seem to hear her.

She understood. This was a vision — as real as it seemed. She could see Connor and hear him, but it was strictly a one-way process. Never mind, this was better than nothing — much better.

It was definitely Connor, though he was wearing someone else's clothes — the clothes of a seafarer. But he seemed happy enough. She watched as he ran over to a broad beam. It was a mast. He was pulling on a rope. She realized that he was hoisting a flag. She looked up and saw the skull and crossbones. Connor was on a pirate ship!

Then the vision grew misty once more. She was losing him. It was over too soon!

"Just a bit longer," she begged. "Please, just a bit longer." But the mist was thickening around her. And then, as it began to thin again, she found herself back in the cabin, holding the broken mirror.

Lorcan was standing before her.

"There now, did you like the captain's gift?"

She nodded, feeling a complete sense of calm and euphoria. "Yes. Yes, I did. Please thank him for me."

"Of course," Lorcan said.

"Tell him . . . tell him that I understand."

Lorcan looked at her quizzically. "You understand? What do you understand, Grace?"

"Everything," she said, smiling softly. "I understand everything now."

Still Lorcan looked puzzled.

"I hardly need explain it to you," she said.

"I think you better had, Grace. I have no idea what you're talking about."

She shook her head, a little amused by his charade.

"What I mean, Lorcan, is that I understand *I'm dead*. I realize now — I drowned that night. You didn't rescue me — not in the conventional sense anyhow. You fished me out of the water and you brought me here. To this . . . this waiting place. But Connor's fine. He's alive. I see that now — the captain let me slip back to look at him, just for a moment. Oh, I feel so happy, Lorcan, I can't tell you. I feel so happy, even though I'm dead!"

14

THE DAWNING

Grace slept more soundly than she could remember. It was strange how being dead felt so much like being alive — but at least she knew now why her sense of time was so distorted. Perhaps it also explained why she was so tired — maybe her mortal body was growing too heavy for her and it would soon to be time to leave it behind.

She opened her eyes and found, to her surprise, that Lorcan was sleeping, slumped over the chair by the port-hole. He had never slept in her cabin before. Was this significant? she wondered. Was she about to pass on from this waiting place? Where was she going? Perhaps, she thought excitedly, her father would be waiting for her there.

What time was it? Grace still had no way of telling

without looking through the porthole. She slipped down from the bed and walked over, past Lorcan, to the curtain. Brushing it carefully to one side, she saw that the darkness was thinning, no longer pitch-black but a smoky gray veil. Dawn must be on its way. But was this the same dawn that greeted the living or were they somewhere else? Grace was eager to find out. If only Lorcan would wake up. She had a whole new raft of questions for him.

Grace let the curtain fall back again. As she did so, the ship lurched in the waves and she lost her footing, stumbling back onto Lorcan. He awoke with a start, a look of panic in his eyes.

"I'm sorry," she said, "I didn't mean to scare you. I tripped."

"How long was I dozing?" he asked.

Grace shrugged. "I don't know. I told you before — I've lost all track of time. But it's starting to get light outside."

"Light?" He looked more panic-stricken than ever.

"Yes, look." She went over to the window and reached for the curtain. The morning was arriving quickly now and the gray veil of a moment ago was lifting, replaced by the deep pinks of sunrise.

Lorcan turned away, as if stung, his hands covering his face.

"What's the matter?" Grace asked. "What's wrong?"

"I shouldn't have slept. I need to be somewhere else."

"Why did you stay here last night?"

"I was worried about you. You seemed feverish. You started talking about being dead."

"But I *am* dead. And I'm not feverish. In fact, I've never been better."

"Grace, you have to listen to me. You are *not* dead."

"I'm not?" Everything had made sense if she was dead, but if she wasn't, it was all as confusing as before.

"How could I have slept through the Dawning Bell?" Lorcan said, holding his head in his hands.

"There was no bell. There can't have been, or it would have woken us both."

Lorcan began trembling. "But Darcy always sounds the bell. How could she have forgotten?"

"Who's Darcy? What's so important about this bell? Are you absolutely sure I'm not dead?"

"I'm one hundred percent sure, Grace. For one thing, dead girls don't eat porridge." He indicated the empty bowl on the tray. "I need to be somewhere else," he said again.

"So go."

Lorcan appeared to be frozen to the spot. "I can't get there in time. I . . ."

He broke off. Clearly frustrated, he pounded the fist of one hand into the palm of the other.

A little perturbed by this show of violence, Grace turned back to the porthole. Lifting the curtain, she looked out through the grimy glass to the pink light of dawn. It was like watching the petals of a flower open.

"Close the curtain, Grace." His voice was hoarse.

"What?"

"Please, Grace, just close the curtain."

She let it fall and turned. His behavior was very strange, especially from someone who had been so cool and collected throughout the short time she had known him. As the curtain fell, Lorcan let out a deep sigh, slowly lowering his hands from his face.

"I'll stay here," he announced at last. "I'll stay with you. That's the best thing."

"That's really kind, but you don't need to worry about me. I'm not feverish — a bit confused perhaps . . ."

"I'm not worried about you."

"Then what? Lorcan, what's the matter?"

He shook his head. "There are things it's better you don't know."

He was still trembling. Now she found herself reaching out a steadying hand to him. Then she had a brain wave. She knew how she could calm him. She opened her mouth and began to sing.

I'll tell you a tale of Vampirates,
A tale as old as true.

Yea, I'll sing you a song of an ancient ship,
And its mighty fearsome crew.
Yea, I'll sing you a song of an ancient ship
That sails the oceans blue . . .
That haunts the oceans blue.

Lorcan's mouth fell open.

"You mean you *know*?" His voice was scarcely more than a whisper.

Grace shook her head, confused. "Know what?"

Lorcan said nothing more, his eyes wide.

"It's a shanty my dad used to sing to Connor and me. It used to calm us whenever we were upset."

Grace smiled and continued her song.

The Vampirate ship has tattered sails
That flap like wings in flight.
They say that the captain, he wears a veil
So as to curtail your fright
At his death-pale skin
And his lifeless eyes
And his teeth as sharp as night.

Oh, they say that the captain, he wears a veil
And his eyes never see the light.

As her voice formed the last words of the verse, both Lorcan and Grace looked toward the porthole. Suddenly, everything became clear to her. It was as if all Lorcan's words had been the scattered pieces of a jigsaw puzzle but now they rose in a swarm and fit themselves together.

And his eyes never see the light. She spoke the words this time, striding back toward the window and taking the curtain in her hand once more.

"No!" Lorcan reached out to catch her.

Too late. Her fingers gripped the corner of the curtain and as Lorcan pulled her away, she tugged at the cloth. It ripped away from the window and a pale streak of light shone into the cabin.

Lorcan released her, covering his eyes again and throwing himself away from the column of light. He cowered in the corner of the cabin.

"Put it back," he whimpered, "put it back. Please, Grace, put the curtain back."

For a moment, Grace was too shocked to do anything but watch him, flailing about like a wasp in a jar. It wasn't a pleasant sight.

But despite the horror of her realization, she couldn't bear to see Lorcan in such distress. So Grace lifted the curtain back over the window. She had torn it clear off its tracks but, holding it there, she was able once more to block out the dawn light.

Lorcan glanced up at her gratefully. "Thank you," he rasped.

"It's okay," Grace said.

She tucked the curtain back over the pole and tied it at both ends. Checking that it still covered the porthole, she turned back to Lorcan.

"Well," she said, "I was *almost* right, wasn't I? Only it isn't *me* that's dead, it's *you*."

He nodded.

"You had better stay here until nightfall, Lorcan Furey. Which will give you plenty of time to explain everything."

She might have sounded like she was in control, but that was about as far as possible from the truth. For now, as she looked at this boy, this handsome boy who appeared to be only a few years older than her, she no longer saw him. For the first time, she saw beyond his long black hair and his sparkling blue eyes. He might be smiling at her now, but soon his mood could change. And behind his soft smile, who knew what dangers lay in wait?

15

CONFLICT

As the days passed on the pirate ship, Connor's hopes and fears ebbed and flowed as frequently as the tide. He clung onto the belief that Grace was alive, that she *had* been rescued by the Vampirate ship and that she was somehow — against all odds — surviving there. Mostly, during the day at least, he could cling onto this belief. But as night fell and he finished the day's chores, dark fears took hold of him.

It was hard to believe that less than a week ago, he and Grace had been living in the lighthouse. And while Connor would do anything to turn back the clock — if it brought Grace back — there was much to be said in favor of life at sea. *The Diablo* was a pretty happy ship, in spite of the tension between Captain Wrathe and Cheng Li.

Connor had made a good friend in Bart. And most of the other pirates were friendly to him, too, though he was always careful to avoid the Stinkbomb and Toothless Jack.

"A bit less thinking and a bit more mopping, please, Connor."

He looked up and caught sight of Cheng Li, marching briskly past, the twin swords jostling on her back. Once again, she'd set him the job of cleaning the deck. He'd groaned inwardly at first but, once he got started on the task, it was no real hardship. It was good to be out in the sunshine, doing something physical and mindless.

"Hey, slowpoke!"

Connor smiled as Bart jumped up beside him. Bart had been given another area of the deck to mop but had clearly made swifter progress.

"Ain't you a slowpoke, Mister Tempest," Bart said, in a joke sneer. "What's the problem? Is the mop a little heavy for ya, newbie?"

"Yeah, right," Connor answered with a smile.

As he removed the mop from the bucket, its head heavy with water, he lifted it and swung it toward Bart, so that his mate received an impromptu shower.

Bart stood dazed for a moment. Connor wondered if he'd overstepped the mark. Bart had an evil look in his eyes. He took his own mop and dipped it in his bucket.

Connor had no time to "reload." Instead, he held out his mop as if it was a sword, readying himself for Bart's strike.

He watched Bart's mop swing toward him but lifted his own to block it. The wooden poles clashed. Water sprayed off them, but Connor stayed dry.

"Bit of a natural, eh?" Bart acknowledged. "Cutlass Cate will be impressed!"

As Bart pulled his mop away, Connor quickly dipped his own mop back in his bucket. Now he was on the offensive. He lunged toward Bart, but Bart blocked the attack, lifting Connor's mop high so that it drenched only Connor. The shock of the water was cold but invigorating. Connor recovered and lunged once more. His mop met Bart's. Bart pulled away. And then they were parrying all along the foredeck, until they reached the very edge of the ship. Bart had the advantage. Connor was pressed against the deckrail.

"Guess I won't make you jump overboard this time, buddy boy," Bart said, a wicked gleam in his eye.

Connor sighed and, with all his strength, raised the mop once more and pushed Bart away.

With a whoop of delight, Bart leaped to respond to the challenge. Once again, they parried across the deck, the mops clashing against each other. Now it was Connor who had the advantage, having maneuvered Bart against a cabin door.

"Ah, you got me!" Bart conceded.

Connor smiled, watching as Bart lowered his mop head. They'd moved at speed across the deck and he was grateful to catch his breath. But as he did so, Bart jumped up and over him. Connor turned to find Bart waiting on the other side of him, mop poised to strike.

"Okay, okay, you win," Connor said, laughing, "but you have to promise you'll teach me that move."

"Sure thing." Bart was a proud victor. "But you did good there, junior. You only made one mistake. Just then. You looked at the mop, when you should have been looking at my eyes. Always watch your opponent's eyes. The sword can lie, but the eyes don't."

With that, he flicked the mop head at Connor and showered him with filthy water.

Above them, they heard the sound of clapping. Blinking through the sunlight and the water in his eyes, Connor looked up and saw Molucco Wrathe leaning over the rail above.

"Very good, lads," he called down. "Me an' Scrimshaw enjoyed the show, didn't we, Scrim? Maybe we'll use mops and brooms on our next raid, eh, Bartholomew?"

"I reckon I'd sooner keep to the broadsword, if that's all right with you, Captain."

"Very good, Bartholomew," said Captain Wrathe. "Now, Mister Tempest, would you be so good as to come up here to my cabin? I'd like a word with you." The captain turned and disappeared back inside.

Bart nudged Connor. "Go on, get a move on! It's never a good idea to keep the captain waiting."

Captain Wrathe's cabin door was open. Connor knocked on the doorjamb.

"Come on in, Mister Tempest."

Connor could hear but not see Captain Wrathe. His cabin appeared to be vast, and was crammed with all manner of objects. This, Connor thought, must be what it was like entering a pharaoh's chamber. A marble statue of an ancient goddess towered over a chest, out of which spilled gold coins and jewels. There were paintings — including one of sunflowers that looked really familiar — propped up against antique chairs.

Further inside, there were twin jeweled baby elephants almost as tall as the real thing. There were mirrors, higher than Connor's head, which doubled the expanse of booty. All this must be plunder Captain Wrathe had amassed on the voyages of *The Diablo,* or perhaps just from his latest voyage. There were clearly some tasty benefits to being a pirate captain.

As Connor stepped deeper into the cabin, he heard music — a strange, haunting melody. Finally, as he peered past a pair of tall Chinese vases, he found Molucco Wrathe, sitting like a sultan of ancient times on a mound of plump silk cushions. Beside him, Scrimshaw was uncurling himself on a bright purple cushion and sliding toward a low table to inspect a plate of honeyed dates.

"You took your time, Mister Tempest," the captain said. "Well, sit yourself down. I'll just turn the music off."

Connor sat down, cross-legged, on a large gold cushion.

"I said, I'll just turn the music off," Captain Wrathe said, more loudly than before.

The captain hadn't moved from his seat — he'd simply raised his voice. The music played on. Connor wasn't sure if he was supposed to do anything.

"Curses," said the captain, reaching around and grabbing an antique warming pan. He turned and brought the head of the pan down hard on something behind him.

The music stopped.

Then there was a moan.

A man fell forward onto the cushions, dropping a sitar at Connor's feet.

"There," said Captain Wrathe, "that's better. I can hear myself think now."

Connor glanced at the concussed sitar player. At least he seemed to still be breathing, Connor noticed with relief.

"Now, to business," Captain Wrathe said, biting into a date and offering the remaining half to Scrimshaw. "How are you taking to life at sea?"

"It's going all right, I think, Captain."

"You must be thinking about your sister and your father an awful lot."

"Yes," Connor said.

"That's as it should be, my boy. Think of them often and give yourself a chance to properly mourn their passing."

Connor nodded, trying not to betray any emotion. Captain Wrathe seemed to have utterly ruled out any possibility that Grace was still alive. For the moment at least, there seemed little point in contradicting him.

"We can never make up for your loss, Mister Tempest, but if you cared to think of us as such, we could be your new family. Not to replace your real one — we could never do that — but all the same to look out for you and give you a place in the world. To reassure you — you are not alone."

Connor was touched, not only by Captain Wrathe's words but by his sensitivity to Connor's feelings.

"Everyone's been really welcoming," Connor said, "Bart, Cutlass Cate, Cheng Li —"

Molucco Wrathe suddenly gripped his neck. His eyes bulged. Was he choking on his date? Connor wasn't sure if he could remember the Heimlich maneuver. He looked around for a glass of water. Then Captain Wrathe burst out laughing.

"Nothing to worry about, dear boy. It's just sometimes the mere mention of Mistress Li gives me a little turn. Curious, eh?"

Connor nodded, smiling and making a mental note to refer to Cheng Li as seldom as possible. Seeing the booty that surrounded them, he found an easy way to change the subject.

"Did you get all this stuff in pirate raids?"

"Abso-blooming-lutely, my boy," Captain Wrathe said proudly. "Most of this is a fresh haul from an attack last week, just a day or two before we made your acquaintance."

"All this is from just one raid?" Connor asked, incredulous.

"Why, yes, but this was an especially successful one. We attacked on land. Got word that the governor's mansion was empty and thought we'd make a little house visit."

Connor was surprised. "I thought pirates only attacked other ships."

Captain Wrathe beamed. "The only rule is that there *are* no rules. It's all about surprise. Do the unexpected. A famous pirate captain of the olden days once said that a pirate's life was a short but merry one. Well, my life has been very merry, though not so short, I'm pleased to say. And I'll drink a cup of rum to that!"

Molucco Wrathe swigged from his tankard. Connor smiled. There was something irresistibly engaging about the captain of *The Diablo*. Piracy seemed to seep from his every pore.

"A short life but a merry one, you hear me, Mister Tempest? There are too many killjoys in the pirate world today, my boy. Persons like Mistress Li, who learned it all from a book — though her father, now, he was a fine pirate. Vicious, though! Hehe, vicious. But, where was I? Yes, there are too many persons who'd learn piracy from a book. They tie themselves up with rules and regulations and petty bureaucracies. But piracy isn't like that. It's about instinct and chance and throwing yourself into danger for the sake of your brother. And we're *all* brothers here. There's an honor to that, d'ya see, my boy? A pirate's honor. And if you bring home the booty, well, why have a frown on your face? Them's only things," he said, sweeping his arm about the cabin. "Pretty paintings, statues, gilded elephants, whatever. They're just things. Last week they were the governor's. And now they're mine. End of story."

"A diamond for your thoughts," Captain Wrathe continued, smiling as he held up a jewel from an open casket. He bit down on it. "Oh, that's rather a good one. I think I might keep it, after all."

"I just want you to know, Captain, how grateful I am . . . for everything." Connor meant it with all his heart.

"Think nothing of it, Mister Tempest. We're all family here. Help yourself to a date. They're Scrimshaw's favorite. We have to take a detour around the Cape to buy them by the barrel, but whatever it takes to keep the little fellow happy . . ." He smiled and nuzzled Scrimshaw again. As much as Connor liked Captain Wrathe, he was finding it a little hard to warm to his beloved reptile.

Connor reached forward and took one of the dates. He could swear that Scrimshaw was fixing him with a look of annoyance. He ate the date somewhat guiltily.

"What do you think of these vases, Mister Tempest? Aren't they beautiful?"

"They're very big," Connor said.

"They were a gift — a peace offering, if you will — from the governor."

"The governor you stole from?"

"Why, yes, dear boy. He sent them over this morning. It's his way of showing there's no hard feelings."

"Isn't that a little strange?"

As Connor finished speaking, he heard a loud chime. He looked up, trying to place the sound. His first thought was that it must be the ship's bell. Was it a call to arms? Captain Wrathe looked equally puzzled. Clearly, he hadn't been expecting the chime. There it was again. Louder.

The chiming continued, regular but growing still louder. And now that it had been repeated, both of them knew that it was not quite the sound a ringing bell makes. Nor was it the chiming of a clock. The sound seemed to be coming from in front of them. But it couldn't be. All that faced them was the pair of tall Chinese vases.

Connor stared at the detailed painting on the vases. A matching scene of a pagoda by a winding river and a tall willow tree and — Suddenly, before his eyes, the vases cracked. The scenes of the pagoda disappeared and the china crumbled away. Out of each vase flew a figure, dressed head to toe in black, each brandishing a weapon.

"What the blazes?" cried Captain Wrathe, as the two intruders dived toward him — one armed with a cutlass, the other with a dagger.

16

UNDER ATTACK

"Who the devil are you? What do you want?" Captain Wrathe asked. If he was scared — and he had every reason to be — he was putting on a good show. But Connor guessed that the captain had stared death in the face many times before.

The two masked men said nothing but drew nearer, hovering before the captain and Connor like large flies.

Then, the one holding the dagger turned to his companion. The cutlass bearer nodded and moved his feet slightly. Now he had both Connor and Captain Wrathe trapped within the sweep of his sword. Connor's heart pounded. If his mop fight with Bart had been Lesson One in combat, here was Lesson Two. And there was a very real possibility that he wouldn't live to see Lesson Three.

The accomplice approached Connor, swiftly running the face of his dagger along either side of Connor's hips. He was checking, Connor realized, for a concealed weapon. Finding none, he moved over to the captain. Captain Wrathe's twin silver scabbards were impossible to miss. The captain had his hand on one, poised to draw it, but he was too slow. In a precise, vicious movement, the dagger bearer cut the scabbards from the captain's belt. They clattered to the floor, narrowly missing Scrimshaw, who slipped forward under the table.

Next, the dagger bearer unwound a band of black cloth from his waist. He threw the cloth at Connor and jerked his head toward the captain. It was clear that he wanted Connor to bind Captain Wrathe with the folds of material.

Connor looked to Captain Wrathe, thinking he'd know what to do. He must have a plan, with all his experience.

But Captain Wrathe simply said, "Best do their bidding, boy. It doesn't pay to argue with metal like that." He held his hands behind his back in readiness.

Did Captain Wrathe have a plan? Was there something Connor could do, like keeping the knots loose? But Molucco Wrathe gave him no clues and the attacker was watching over him too closely not to bind the knots securely. Sadly, he wrapped the length of cloth about the captain's wrists. After he had completed the task, the man held the tip of the dagger toward him and, obediently, Connor stepped backward as the aggressor inspected the bindings. He appeared to be satisfied.

Turning, he ran the dagger's tip across the pile of cushions in front of Connor and the captain. A mist of feathers rose into the air as the blade cut through the skin of the cushion covers.

As the feathers rose, Connor sneezed and slightly lost his footing. He steadied himself but felt something digging into his lower back. It was the handle of the warming pan the captain had used to take a swipe at the sitar player earlier. Connor let the handle push into the hollow of his spine, wondering if there was some way he could grab the pan.

The attacker scooped up Molucco Wrathe's fallen scabbards from the floor. He pushed one into his own belt loop and removed the cutlass from the other, throwing it to his companion. His accomplice caught it expertly. Now he menaced them with a cutlass in each hand.

The feathers had fallen down over the cushions and table and lay there like drifts of snow. The man with the dagger moved off into the depths of the cabin. Connor realized that his splicing of the cushions might not have been a random act of vandalism. He appeared to be hunting for something.

Though Connor was not bound like Captain Wrathe, he was still powerless to move with the cutlass bearer hovering in readiness before him. He remembered Bart's advice.

Always watch your opponent's eyes. The sword can lie, but the eyes don't. He looked from the tips of the ferocious blades into his opponent's eyes. They were deep brown, he noticed. Connor looked beyond the color and he saw, to his surprise, a flash of fear.

Careful not to show any obvious response, Connor dropped his gaze. Could it be that his attacker, though possessed of not one but two deadly sharp blades, was scared? Was he scared of what might happen? Too scared to use them? The pan handle was digging into Connor's back and a plan was beginning to form. It all depended upon seizing his moment.

Meanwhile, the other adversary was causing chaos within the cabin. Connor could hear the treasures he'd glimpsed on the way in crashing to the floor — paintings torn, chairs roughly broken. He could only imagine the extent of the damage being done.

During all this commotion, neither he, Captain Wrathe, nor their attacker with the cutlasses moved. It was as if they were held in a delicate bubble of stillness and silence.

An ornate mirrored screen crashed to the floor, showering shards of glass across the deck. Once more, Connor feared for Scrimshaw's safety, but he had other concerns now. The vandal was once more visible to Connor and the others. Stepping over the sea of glass, the man approached the marble statue of the goddess. His dark eyes twinkling, the attacker raised his dagger to the statue's throat. Was this a warning? Connor could see in this man's eyes no fear, no hesitation. He watched as the man made the action of slitting the statue's throat. Connor winced.

As the blade touched the marble, a strange thing happened. A streak of red appeared beneath the blade. Connor flinched as, wide-eyed, the brute ran his knife back along the statue's neck. What was going on? What secrets did the statue hide?

The man with the dagger lost no time in finding out. He jammed the dagger into the cut and somehow managed to slice off the statue's head. As it fell to the ground and smashed, a fountain of red spurted from the beheaded statue and showered over his feet. It had been filled with rubies.

This was clearly what the man had been looking for. He unclipped a black bag from his waist and, slipping his dagger back under his waistband, began scooping the jewels into the bag.

His cutlass-bearing comrade looked over his shoulder to get a better view. As he did so, very slowly and carefully, Connor brought his hand behind him and, his eyes still on the cutlass bearer, reached out for the pan handle.

Out of the corner of his eye, Connor saw Scrimshaw slip out from under the table and glide off in the direction of the attackers. What was the snake up to?

He knew the minute that Scrimshaw coiled himself

about the cutlass bearer's legs. He saw it in the man's eyes, and Connor lost no time in seizing the moment. His fingers found the handle of the warming pan the captain had used before. He grasped it tightly.

The attacker, with the snake coiling around his ankle, cried out, his words muffled under his mask. At the cry, his companion turned. His hands were brimming over with rubies, their red glow reflected in his dark eyes.

Connor swung the pan around and, letting out a warrior's roar, spun it through the air and down onto the man's head. The metal base made heavy contact and the man fell, dazed, onto a pile of rubies. He was out cold.

Meanwhile, his cohort was trying to flick Scrimshaw off his leg with the tip of a cutlass.

"No," the captain cried. "Leave Scrimshaw alone!"

Connor lifted the dagger from the fallen attacker's waistband and seized back Captain Wrathe's stolen scabbard. There was no time to draw it, so he tucked it under his own belt.

The man with the cutlasses was frantically trying to shake Scrimshaw off his leg. His eyes bulged with terror and his attention was scattered. It was easy for Connor to swing the dagger and knock the first cutlass out of his hand.

But this seemed to awaken the man. And, as scared as he might be at having a snake slowly but surely crush his lower leg, he turned to face Connor with the remaining cutlass. Connor could not waste time removing Captain Wrathe's sword from its scabbard. But he had the dagger.

He looked into the would-be-assassin's eyes and could tell that, in spite of the man's pose, his opponent was still flushed with fear. Connor hesitated, not wanting to endanger Scrimshaw. If the attacker fell, he might crush the snake. It was strange having to fight alongside a reptile, but Connor decided that he had to carry on with the attack. Scrimshaw had bravely offered himself up to save the captain, and now it was up to Connor to finish the job.

He raised the dagger and moved it through the air in front of him, getting a feel for its weight and the speed at which he could turn it.

The attacker struck out with his remaining cutlass. Fearlessly Connor parried. Metal clashed against metal and, although the cutlass was bigger, Connor's grip on his dagger was stronger. The cutlass trembled in his opponent's hand. Quickly withdrawing the dagger, Connor swung it back against the blade. The sword slipped out of the man's hand. Connor jumped forward and seized it triumphantly. Now he had the cutlass in his right hand and the dagger in his left.

His opponent reached down toward the first fallen cutlass. But as he stooped low to retrieve the weapon, he didn't notice a diminutive musician move up behind him.

Soon a sitar string bound him around the waist and arms. He was trapped.

Scrimshaw uncoiled himself from the man's ankle and wriggled back across the feather-covered floor toward his master.

"Good work, lads," Captain Wrathe said, as Connor freed him.

Molucco Wrathe scooped up Scrimshaw with one hand and the fallen cutlass with the other. "That's a fine bit of teamwork if ever I saw it. A very fine bit of teamwork, indeed!"

17

THE VAMPIRE

Grace's heart was racing. She stood by the porthole, touching the curtain. Lorcan sat in the chair on the other side of the cabin. It was a fair compromise. He swore that he wouldn't attack her, but how could she be sure, knowing what she now knew? As long as she held the curtain, she bought herself some fragile kind of safety. If he so much as moved toward her, she would expose the light again and force him to retreat once more.

It was weird thinking of him in this way. He looked about as far from being a monster as could be. He was her ally, the one who'd saved her life. Could he really intend her harm? Could he really be a . . . a . . . She couldn't even bring herself to frame the word yet.

"How old are you?" she asked instead.

"I'm seventeen," he said, "but I thought you knew that already."

"What year were you born?"

"Ah." He smiled, nodding but not answering.

"What year, Lorcan? I need to know."

"1803."

"So, in fact, you're, you're seven hundred and nine years old!"

"It doesn't work like that, Grace. It's hard to explain. I'm seventeen. That's the age I was when I crossed. And that's the age I'll always be."

"But you *have* been roaming this earth, these seas for over six centuries?"

"Time moves very differently on this side," Lorcan said quietly, "though truth to tell, I've lost much sense of what it was like before."

"You've forgotten your life?"

He shook his head.

"Far from it. I remember the facts of my life well enough. I remember my time in Dublin and all that happened to me. I remember how it ended. But it's like a story someone told me over and over again. I know every last detail but I don't remember how it felt to be alive."

Grace looked at the boy before her, just four years older than her by one measure, and yet a world away by another. It was hard to take in.

"When you cross over," he explained, "you lose the old

rhythms. I can walk and talk like before. I can help to sail a fine ship, such as this. But I cannot feel the things you feel. It's hard to describe, Grace. What I'd give to feel for a moment what you feel. Even your pain would be better than this numbness."

Grace frowned. What did he know of her pain? If he'd care to change places with her, she was ready to consider it.

Her anger soon dissolved as she noticed a strange expression passing across his face. Just for a moment, he did not look like the Lorcan she knew. His eyes seemed as empty as the eyes of a statue, his nostrils flared, and as his mouth opened, she caught sight of an uncommon sharpness to one of his teeth. Grace shivered. He looked like the other one — Sidorio. Then it hit her. There were others like him on board. Many others.

Lorcan shook slightly and his features smoothed back into their regular shape. He looked up at her with those familiar eyes, as if nothing had happened. Where had he gone to in that strange moment? She dared not ask him.

"I shouldn't be telling you these things," Lorcan said.

"Will you be punished? What will the captain do?"

"The captain is a fair man," Lorcan said. "I haven't been on this crew very long, and I don't know him that well. He isn't someone you get to know well. But he treats us all fairly. He has a very special vision. Since I crossed, I've been to terrible places, places of darkness such as I hope you'll never see. But I'm safe now. This ship is my harbor."

"Am *I* safe?" The words slipped out before she had a chance to censor them.

"From me? Yes, Grace, you're safe. I swore it before and I'll swear it again, I'll never do you harm."

She wanted to believe him. She thought she could trust him. Still, she kept a tight hold on the curtain.

"But am I safe from the others?"

Lorcan did not look up, but reached into his pocket and produced a gold key on a long chain. He let it swing back and forth as if hypnotizing her.

"Why do you think you've been kept under lock and key in the cabin beside the captain's?"

She had no answer. She watched the key swing back and forth, wondering what it would take to grab it and run. If she pulled back the curtain, he'd soon drop it. That would give her enough time . . .

"Maybe you've been locked up not to keep *you* in, but to keep *others* out."

His words froze her. They made sense. How many more of them were out there?

Lorcan tucked the key and chain back into his pocket. "Things are not always as they seem, Grace. But I have a suspicion you already knew that. The captain has ordered me to protect you. That's why you're in this cabin — that's why you cannot go out yet."

"But what does the captain want from me? I don't understand."

"That I don't know, Grace. I'm just following my orders."

A moment ago, she had felt safe, reassured. Now she felt more under threat than ever. Lorcan could talk the talk, but he had no real power. Her fate was in the hands of the captain.

"I want to see him," she announced.

"To see who?"

"The captain. Will you bring him to me?"

Lorcan laughed. "Haven't I already made that plain? Nobody but nobody summons the captain, Grace. He'll see you when he decides he's good and ready."

"No," Grace said. "I've waited long enough. I want to see him. Either ask him to come to me here, or take me to him. Now."

Her breath was coming fast now. She had to find a quick resolution to this.

"Even if I wanted to, I couldn't," Lorcan said. "Not while it's light. The ship sleeps through the day. When the Dawning Bell sounds, the decks clear and everyone takes shelter. Even the captain."

"But the Dawning Bell didn't sound. You said so yourself." Grace was thinking on her feet.

"Yes, but it matters not. I don't know why Darcy failed to sound it, but it doesn't change anything. None but the captain can walk beneath the sun."

Grace thought for a moment.

"*You* can't go out there, it's true, but *I* can. If you give me the key, I can go and find the captain myself. You said his cabin's right next door."

Lorcan shook his head.

"I'm not giving you this key, Grace. I'm sorry."

She frowned at him and he stared back stubbornly.

"I thought you were my friend," she said.

"That's a low blow, Grace. I've done what I can for you. I've swum the icy waters for you. I've pleaded your case with the captain. And now I've risked my own safety and reputation by staying here with you. But now I must obey orders."

Grace folded her arms across her chest and bit her lip in frustration. She tasted blood again. The rest happened in a blur. Suddenly, Lorcan was standing before her, his eyes gazing down into hers more intently than ever. His hand reached out for hers and she realized she had let go of the curtain. There was no escaping his grip now, as he turned her palm upward. Then she felt the coldness of metal as he pressed the key into her flesh.

"Go," he said. "Go now, before . . . before I change my mind."

He turned away and covered his eyes. His hands were trembling.

Grace felt the weight of the key and its snaking chain in her hand. She looked toward the door.

18

PUNISHMENT TO FIT THE CRIME

"And now let us unmask the villains," announced Captain Wrathe to his excited crew.

The two intruders had been securely bound and led down from the devastation of Captain Wrathe's cabin to the main deck. They gave little resistance, and Connor could see the fear and resignation in their eyes.

An attack on the captain was a major event, and the whole crew ceased their labors to see who had perpetrated the evil scheme. The pirates pressed forward noisily, jostling for position until Molucco Wrathe raised his hand and begged for silence. His request was granted immediately — no one was in a mood to defy the captain.

"Mister Connor Tempest, why don't you do the honors?"

He gave Connor a gentle nudge forward, toward the two prisoners.

"Remove their hoods and let us see who these villains are," continued the captain.

Connor stood before the two attackers. Their hands had been roughly drawn behind their backs and their bodies were tightly bound from their chests to their knees. How different they looked now from when they'd menaced him and Captain Wrathe with the dagger and cutlass.

"What are you waiting for?" cried a rough pirate voice.

"Get on with it, boy!" cried another.

Captain Wrathe silenced the crowd again. Connor stepped forward and lifted the two hoods, stepping back to give the audience a better view.

The faces revealed to the crowd at large what Connor had realized much earlier. His two attackers were young men, probably only two or three years older than himself. They'd had guts to board *The Diablo* and hide in the giant vases, biding their time. They'd done well to get past Captain Wrathe's many protectors.

"I recognize you two," the captain said, drawing nearer. "There's something familiar in those faces."

"Cut off their noses!" cried one of the pirates.

"No, slit their ears!" shouted another.

Connor could see that one of the boys was saying something, though his voice was drowned out by the din.

"He's trying to speak," he said to Captain Wrathe.

Again the captain raised a hand toward the crew, though the calls to punish the intruders were growing more persistent and imaginative.

"Come on," Captain Wrathe said, "if you have something to say, boy, spit it out fast. I can't keep this mob silent for long."

"We're from Port Hazzard," the boy said. "Our father's the governor there. You pillaged our house and we came to teach you a lesson."

Connor was impressed by the boy's fire, even in such dismal circumstances. It seemed that Captain Wrathe was, too. "You came to teach *me* a lesson, eh? Tell us more. We're all ears. Go on, boy, we're all waiting."

"Stick to the seas," said the boy, fiercely. "You may have dominion here, but the land is ours."

There were more cries from the mob. Connor could see that the other boy was close to tears. Clearly, he did not share his brother's venom. Connor recognized him as the younger of the pair, the one who'd wielded the cutlasses. He had shown flair in his swordsmanship but his eyes had betrayed his lack of confidence.

"You had better let us go," the older brother now told Captain Wrathe.

"Had I now? Why is that, I wonder? Do you have another dagger concealed in your sock or an extending cutlass behind your ear, perhaps? And if you do, how, pray tell, do you intend to reach them?"

"Dump 'em in the soup!" cried one of the mob.

"String them from the rigging!" Connor recognized Bart's voice.

"If," continued the boy proudly, "anything happens to my brother and me, our father will send out a force such as you have never seen before. You and your crew will be massacred. And even if you sail away up the Cape, we have friends in the northern territory, too. If you kill us, you will sign your own death warrant with our blood."

The mere mention of death and blood proved too much for the younger brother, who threw up on the deck, narrowly missing the back of Captain Wrathe's velvet coat.

"This *is* interesting," Captain Wrathe said, stepping forward and keeping his attention on the cockier of the pair. "There may be something in what you say."

The boy looked triumphantly at the captain and Connor. Connor remembered how the rubies had reflected in his unnaturally dark eyes.

"I don't reckon I shall kill you," Captain Wrathe said.

There was uproar from the crew.

"Hold on, hold on. I haven't finished. I don't reckon we'll kill you *just yet*. I'm going to have to think about this one. And while I'm exercising my brain cells, I reckon we'll follow Mister Bartholomew's suggestion and string this third-rate pair from the rigging."

A huge wave of cheering arose from the crowd. The captain called forward Bartholomew and some of his mates. As the nastier of the two brothers was roughly dragged away, he spat in Connor's direction.

Then he disappeared from view, along with his brother, who seemed in danger of throwing up again. Connor felt a certain pity toward the younger boy. Odds were he had been bullied into the attack by his more forceful sibling.

It did not take long for Bart and his fellows to do their work. Within minutes, the boys had been trussed up and were swinging through the air upside down from the mast, like joints of meat in a butcher's window.

The crew cheered and shouted insults at the pair as they swung back and forth overhead.

In their excitement, few were aware of the figure climbing the ladder on the side of the ship and leaping athletically onto the deck.

"What on earth is going on?" cracked a voice like breaking thunder.

It was Cheng Li — her face as dark as storm clouds, her eyes sparking like lightning. Connor had been too caught up in events to notice her absence before. He wondered where she had been.

"Ah, Mistress Li, welcome back," said Captain Wrathe.

Cheng Li pushed her way through the crowd. "Go back to your business," she shouted to the pirates. "Back to your tasks, I say."

There was a significant amount of grumbling but the mob gradually began to disperse.

Cheng Li stood before Captain Wrathe, her face still flushed with fury. "Do you know who those boys are?" she said.

"Yes, Mistress Li, I do. They are evil little beggars who but one hour ago had their swords trained on young Mister Tempest and I and, but for the lad's ingenuity and bravery, might have sliced our guts out."

"Is this true?" Cheng Li turned her face to Connor.

"Don't turn away from me!" thundered Molucco Wrathe. "Forgive me, Mistress Li, but have I missed something? Have you taken over command of *The Diablo*? Because, when I last looked at the ship's log, it still read Captain Molucco Wrathe."

Connor was shocked at Captain Wrathe's fury. Evidently, Cheng Li was, too, for when she next spoke, her tone was much softer. "I apologize, Captain. I spoke in haste. But for your own good — for all our good — those boys are Governor Acharo's sons. Acharo has always been lenient with pirates in the waters adjacent to his land. Any harm we do to them will come back to us a hundred-fold."

"I'm fully aware of this, Mistress Li, and I do not intend any lasting harm to be done. We shall give them a scare and then we shall dispatch them — though the crew are justly baying for their blood. Strangely, it seems my crew take issue with their captain being attacked in his own cabin."

Cheng Li opened her mouth to speak again but Captain Wrathe had not finished.

"And it certainly calls into question our security measures, Mistress Li, doesn't it? I seem to remember when you drew up that rather tedious workbook on shipboard security that it was to be your responsibility."

Again Cheng Li began to speak but Captain Wrathe cut her off, as brutally as if he'd sliced a sword through her words.

"It is because of this boy," he said, throwing his arm about Connor, "and this boy *alone* that I am alive and standing before you. While you were off having tea and biscuits and a bit of a chin-wag at the Pirate Academy, this lad risked his life to save mine. *That's* what being a pirate is about. I feel sure your father would have agreed with me. Now you wait until those lads up there are feeling just a little too giddy and then you send them packing with a warning to Governor Acharo and *any other* have-a-go heroes along the Cape: Attack Captain Molucco Wrathe and his crew and there'll be hell to pay."

Cheng Li closed her mouth. Clearly, this was no time to talk back to Molucco Wrathe. Instead, she nodded so low it was almost a bow and made her exit.

Once she was out of hearing, Molucco Wrathe turned to Connor and gave him a wink. "I've been wanting to say some of those things for a long while now. I feel purged, my lad, purged!"

Connor couldn't help but smile.

"As for you, young sir, what bravery, what instinct! Now

you must name your reward. Whatever your heart desires shall be yours."

There was nothing Connor wanted more than to find Grace. He needed to find a way to trace the Vampirate ship — rather than just waiting and hoping. The captain hadn't taken him seriously before but now perhaps he would. But it was a gamble. He didn't want to see the captain unleash on him the fury he'd directed at Cheng Li.

"Come on, boy, out with it. Anything your heart desires."

Connor's heart began beating faster. He was scared but he had to give it one more try.

"Please, Captain Wrathe. I need your help to find my sister."

"Your sister?" Captain Wrathe frowned. "But, my boy, your sister cannot be found. I wish she could, oh I wish it with all my heart, but alas . . ."

"I know you don't believe that there's a Vampirate ship," Connor said, unable to let this chance go. "But even if there isn't, Captain, I feel she's still alive. We're twins and we're close. I can't explain the feeling that I have but I just know she's alive."

Captain Wrathe looked at him sadly. "Mister Tempest, are you sure that you feel it? Or is it perhaps that you just wish it to be so?"

The captain's tone was incredibly gentle. It brought

Connor up sharp. Suddenly, all his excitement and deter-mination drained away. He'd got through these days on the pirate ship, clinging onto the belief that Grace was alive — that somehow he'd find her. But what if she wasn't? What if she really had drowned that first night? Maybe he *had* only hallucinated that ship with the strange winglike sails — as clear as the vision had seemed. Perhaps it was time to accept that Grace was not coming back and to get on with his life. His life as a pirate.

"I'm sorry, Connor. Truly I am. I can make inquiries about this Vampirate ship, if you wish. But I'd be lying to you if I said I thought there was any purpose in that, and I don't lie to my friends, my brothers."

Connor nodded, once more having to bite back tears. This was it, then. He was alone. His father and Grace had gone. He was an orphan. A pirate orphan. Suddenly, he had a flash of inspiration.

"Captain Wrathe, I'll tell you what I'd like as my re-ward. I would like sword-fighting lessons."

Molucco Wrathe beamed. "A fine answer, my boy, a fine answer! I sensed the blood of a pirate in you the first moment I clapped eyes on you and then again in my cabin back there. A lesson, it is. And from our finest tutor — Cutlass Cate. I shall inform her immediately."

Molucco Wrathe strode off purposefully, beaming from ear to ear.

Connor walked up the guardrail and looked out to the distant horizon. Truly it seemed to stretch out toward infinity.

"I'm doing this for you, Grace," he said softly, "and for you, Dad. I'm going to make you both proud of me. I'm going to be the best pirate that ever sailed the sea. And I'm never going to forget you. I'm never going to forget either of you."

As he stood there, desperately trying to say good-bye, he felt his sister's presence more strongly than ever. Then something strange happened. Inside his head, he heard a voice. His dad's voice.

"Don't let her go, Connor. Not now. Not now when she needs you the most."

"It's too hard," Connor said, as though his dad were standing next to him. "I want to help, but I don't know how. I don't know what to do or how to find her."

His eyes were streaming. Furiously, he blinked away his tears. Then he heard his dad's voice again, even clearer than before.

"Make yourself ready, Connor. That's all. Make yourself ready. Trust the tide."

Make yourself ready. Trust the tide. What did he mean? Why was he talking in riddles?

"What do you mean, Dad? What do I have to do?"

He waited, wanting to hear him again. Could it *really* be his father? It *had* to be, thought Connor. It didn't even matter what he said — just hearing the soft, familiar voice was reward enough. How he had missed it. But try as he might to summon its return, all he heard now was the rumble of the ocean and the cawing of gulls overhead.

At last he turned and walked back across the deck. His head was spinning but, for now, he had chores to do. The afternoon's events had kept him from his pirate duties.

19

THE CAPTAIN

Grace opened the door only a touch, to contain the amount of light coming into the cabin. As quickly as she could, to reduce Lorcan's discomfort, she wriggled out of the small gap and closed the door behind her. Being out in the air, after so long cooped up in the cabin, was a heady sensation. She closed her eyes as she inhaled deep breaths of fresh air, made even more refreshing by the smell of sea salt. Even before she opened her eyes, she could feel the heat of the sun on her face — as gentle as a feather at first, then stronger.

Glancing from left to right, she saw the red-painted decks were quite empty, just as Lorcan had said they'd be. She walked up to the guardrail and looked out to the horizon. It was perfect weather. The sea was calm and its crystal surface seemed to dance with light as it reflected back the sun's rays.

At first it seemed a magical sight, made all the more so by having it to herself, but then Grace's thoughts turned. The sea might be calm and majestic in the morning light, but when she'd last seen it, it had been a very different story. The waters that appeared so restful and alluring now were the same waters that had roughly broken her and Connor's boat in two and hungrily dragged her and her brother down into its depths.

Feeling suddenly giddy, Grace turned away, leaning against the guardrail for support. As she opened her eyes, she caught her breath. She was standing before the cabin next to hers. Her heart missed a beat. Was this the captain's cabin? It must be, for these two cabins were separated from the others. As she looked at the heavy wood door, it opened with a creak. She found herself frozen to the spot. She had wanted to speak to the captain for so long. But now, suddenly, she felt unsure of herself. She knew that this was no ordinary ship, so what did that make the captain? What demon lay beyond the dark gap in the doorway?

"Won't you come inside?"

As before, the voice was only a whisper but the words were perfectly clear — as if they came not from deep inside the cabin but from inside Grace's own head. Instinctively, she stepped toward the door and crossed over the threshold. Her eyes were met only by darkness. The door closed behind her, seemingly of its own accord.

"Welcome, Grace. Come in."

Again, the words were whispered. Again, they seemed to be spoken inside her own head. But though it was only a whisper, the voice was commanding. The contrast between the light outside and the dark within temporarily blinded her, but as Grace walked farther forward, she began to see through the veil of darkness.

It was hard to get a sense of the size of the cabin as her sight could not yet pinpoint its corners. But in the center was a round polished wooden table, strewn with charts and an array of navigational instruments. In the center of the table, an oil lamp burned low. It appeared to be the sole source of light in the room.

Though the lamp lit the circle of the table, beyond its edges the rest of the cabin was still shrouded in darkness. She looked down into the pool of golden light. Some of the navigational instruments looked familiar to her. Others were new and curious. Beneath them, the map itself was richly illustrated. She scanned the artwork, looking for a familiar stretch of coast.

She heard his voice. "Please come and join me."

"Where are you?"

"I'm out here, of course. Where else?"

At these words, the light in the room shifted. Two thick curtains separated and lifted and Grace found herself facing a panel of shuttered doors, through which daylight filtered.

Then the doors folded back on themselves and she saw a dark figure standing on a balcony, his gloved hands fixed on a vast wooden steering wheel.

"Please, try not to be alarmed by my appearance."

Tentatively, Grace walked outside to join him at the wheel.

Above the gloves, the captain's arms disappeared into the folds of a dark, multilayered cape, made of thin leather. Grace's eyes traced up to his neck, where the cape fanned out in a jagged ruff and was fastened by a chain of black gemstones. And then she glimpsed his face. Or rather, the space where his face might have been. For in its place was a mesh mask. She could see nothing beneath the mask, but it was shaped to the contours of a face, with indentations for the eyes and mouth. It fitted as perfectly as a death mask but was not as rigid. It couldn't be because, as she gazed at it, the mask creased on either side of the mouth indentation. Grace realized with a shock that the captain might be smiling at her.

"You must have expected something like this."

Grace was speechless.

. . . they say that the captain, he wears a veil
And his eyes never see the light . . .

It was strange to hear the words in the captain's rich, resonant whisper.

"I dispensed with the veil some years ago. I find this mask more . . . practical."

The back of the captain's head was closely shaven and Grace could see that far from being deathly pale, his skin was a deep brown color. The mask was fastened by three leather straps: two extending from each ear to the center; the third reaching down over the crown of his head. The three straps met in a buckle, shaped like a pair of silver wings, in the center of his head.

"But why . . . why do you cover your face at all?" Grace asked.

The query slipped from her mouth instinctively. In the silence that followed, she began to regret the question and to fear the coming whisper.

"Why do *you* think?"

The obvious answer lay in the shanty.

They say that the captain, he wears a veil
So as to curtail your fright
At his death-pale skin

And his lifeless eyes
And his teeth as sharp as . . .

". . . but your skin *isn't* death-pale."

The captain nodded, turning the wheel slightly.

"So maybe the rest isn't true, either," Grace said.

He did not answer but waited, watching her.

Suddenly, Grace felt a shooting pain in her head. At the same time, she had a fleeting vision of a tearing of flesh and a flash of crimson blood on dark skin. It was a horrible sight, but in an instant it was gone and she was looking at the captain's mask again.

Who *was* this monster behind the mask? Maybe he wasn't human at all. Maybe he never had been.

The shooting pain returned, this time more strongly. Grace closed her eyes, partly for relief and partly to avoid witnessing the horror she'd seen before. But, eyes open or closed, there was no escape. Once more, the sudden tearing of flesh and a flash of crimson on dark skin. And then it was gone.

The pain disappeared along with the image, but Grace felt numb and a little giddy from it. Opening her eyes again, she looked back at the captain's strange, eyeless gaze.

Nothing had changed. But this time she did not see a demon.

"Are you covering up a wound?" she asked hesitantly.

For an instant, there was no response, then the captain nodded slowly.

"Very good, Grace. You are as exceptional as I might have expected. While others see only the mask, you see beyond."

Again the captain appeared to be smiling at her.

"So, we meet at last."

The whisper was not without warmth, but it was not enough to stem the tide of Grace's fears.

"What is it that you want from me?" she asked, no longer able to hold back the question that burned inside her.

"What do *I* want from *you*?" came the slow, deliberate reply. "Grace, it was *you* who sought *me* out, was it not?"

It was true. Grace had sought out the captain in his cabin. She had wanted answers and Lorcan seemed to have run out of those.

"Let's go inside," he said.

"But what about . . . the wheel?"

The captain had already brushed past her and gone into his cabin. Grace stood out on the balcony, dumbfounded. Before her, the wheel continued turning — a touch to the left, a little to the right — as though the captain's hands were still upon it.

20

SAFE HAVEN

Grace followed the captain back inside. Behind her the shuttered doors closed themselves and the dark curtains slammed back together.

"What makes you think I want anything from you?" The captain's whisper swirled in Grace's head.

Grace considered the question as she searched for him in the darkness.

"It's just a feeling I have. You told Lorcan to tell me that Connor was safe. And then you locked me away in that cabin, and assigned Lorcan to protect me — or so he says at any rate."

"Midshipman Furey speaks the truth."

"Well, then," said Grace, realizing that he had sat down at the map table, "it seems to me there are two possibilities.

Either you're protecting me from some danger on board this ship, or else you have some other purpose in mind for me. Maybe both." She looked directly into the captain's mask, wishing she could see his eyes.

The captain nodded. "Come — sit with me if you will."

She did as he commanded, her eyes falling from his mask to his cape. Now that she looked more closely, she saw that the material was not leather, as she had first thought. It seemed lighter and the lamplight illuminated thin veins running through it. The veins appeared to soak up the light, making the cloak glow. Grace would have liked to touch it, to see how it felt, but she did not dare.

"Let us suppose you are right, Grace. What dangers might I be protecting you from? And what purpose do you suppose I might have with you?"

No wonder Lorcan spoke in riddles, with a captain like this. Clearly, this was the way of the ship. No matter — she would play the captain's game. It would not further her cause to displease him.

"I know what you are," she said. "I don't know how many other vampires there are on board, but my guess is quite a number. And vampires need blood, don't they?"

The captain nodded. "In most circumstances, yes, they do."

This was interesting. What did he mean by "most circumstances"?

"Do you think we're after your blood, Grace?"

There couldn't be any other real possibility, could there — no matter how kind Lorcan had appeared, no matter how carefully the captain now framed his words. This was a ship of vampires. She was nothing to them but a fresh supply of blood. The very thought of it made her shiver.

"The fact is," continued the captain, "that the . . . crew are well catered to in that department. If you choose to stay with us a little longer, you will see what I mean. I think you'll find it most . . . enlightening."

If you choose. That was an interesting choice of words. Did she *have* a choice in the matter?

"How much do you know about this ship?" the captain asked her.

"Very little. I wanted to leave my cabin, but Lorcan wouldn't let me."

"Perhaps he *was* being a little overprotective, but he had your best interests at heart."

"So I *am* in danger then?"

"A new arrival is bound to provoke interest."

She wasn't exactly sure what he meant, but something in his tone made her halt this line of inquiry.

"You're naturally curious, aren't you?" the captain said at length. "It's what I should have expected. A child as bright as you would never be content to be shut in a cabin, all alone."

Grace was not at ease with compliments but she nodded.

It was true. The last thing she wanted was to be shut back in the cabin. She wanted to explore the ship.

"There's certainly no reason you can't leave your cabin," the captain told her, "but it would be safer not to go above deck after Miss Flotsam sounds the Nightfall Bell."

"Why?" Grace asked. "What happens then?"

"It's when the ship comes to life. There are many tasks that the crew must attend to. We have only the hours of darkness to work in. They must have no distractions from their work."

"I've seen people outside sometimes, Captain, but they must be very quiet most of the time or I'd have noticed them."

The captain smiled again. "Yes, you've been looking out of that porthole quite a bit, haven't you? Again, I should have expected that. But you've also been sleeping a lot, Grace, and sleeping rather deeply."

"It's the food," she said. "I know there is something in the food. Have you been drugging me?"

"No," the captain said, "at least not in the conventional sense. It's complicated."

"Was it you who delivered the food to my cabin? And the candles — do you bring the candles back to life?"

"So many questions," the captain said. "There's no rush to know all this, is there, my child? There's always time. I know what I'm talking about. There's always time."

"So it's fine for me to wander around the deck alone

during the day, when all the crew but you are asleep. But once you are up, I must scurry back inside like a mouse?"

"Fascinating," said the captain. "What a brave child you are. Doesn't it scare you, being surrounded by people like me?"

"My dad always comforted us with the Vampirate shanty," Grace said. "He said that whatever was scaring us, nothing could be so bad as a Vampirate. But now, after everything I've been through these past days, even you don't seem so scary."

"Even with my mask and this cape? Even though you think I want your blood?"

"Do you *want* me to be scared?"

"Far from it, Grace. You're a guest aboard my ship. I want you to feel at home."

Grace couldn't help but smile. "Home? Here?"

"This ship has been sailing for a very long time," the captain said. "It's a refuge, Grace, a safe haven — for outsiders, for those of us forced, or drawn, to the very edges of the world."

The captain paused, giving Grace a chance to contemplate his words, before continuing.

"I think *you* are an outsider, Grace. I don't think you have ever quite fit in. It's true, isn't it? For Connor, too."

Grace was taken aback. And not just at the mention of Connor. The captain seemed to know so much about the two of them. It was true — the Tempest twins *had* always been misfits. But how did the captain know? Had he been watching them? If so, from where? And for how long? He seemed to know even their most private thoughts. Or was it a trick? Her mind ached from all the possibilities.

"I wish Connor was here now," she said at last.

The captain nodded. "He'll be with us soon. Did you like your gift?"

"The vision of him? Yes, yes, I did. It confused me, but it was great to see him."

"You shall see him again, my child, for real."

"Where is he, Captain? Is he on a pirate ship? Is he close by?"

"Ah, such a lot of questions. He is safe, Grace. Connor is coping very well — as are you. You do your father great credit."

"Our father," Grace said. "Do you know him?"

There was a long pause.

"I'm afraid I'm growing tired, my child. We will talk again, but for now I must rest."

He rose from his seat and approached a rocking chair, in front of a fire she had not noticed before. Perhaps because it was merely glowing embers. The captain sat down in the rocking chair, arranging the folds of his cape over its sides.

"It was nice meeting you at last, Grace," he said, before leaning his head forward. She realized she had been dismissed.

21

SWORDS

For the first time since arriving on *The Diablo,* Connor slept well. Hearing his father's voice had calmed him deeply. Somehow it had allowed him to let go of the constant torment of what to believe and what to do. *Make yourself ready. Trust the tide.* He had kept repeating those words as he'd drifted off to sleep. It didn't matter what the others thought. Grace was still alive. His feeling had been right all along.

"Hey, buddy, wake up! Shake a tail!"

Connor opened his eyes to find Bart already dressed, shaved, and buzzing with energy.

"What time is it?" Connor asked. "Did I miss breakfast?"

"Nah, buddy, it's early. But did you forget? It's your first sword-fighting class this morning. Get your gear on. We don't want to keep Cate waiting!"

"What's that smell?" Connor wrinkled his nose.

Bart blushed.

Connor smiled. "Are you wearing cologne . . . for Cate?"

"I just thought I'd freshen up. Now get a move on, mate."

Less than ten minutes later, after the quickest of washes, Connor and Bart arrived on the foredeck. Cutlass Cate was busy laying out an array of weaponry. She was friendly but businesslike, her red hair twisted back in a neat ponytail and covered by her customary bandanna. Her eyes were bright with energy and purpose as she pulled on a pair of leather gloves.

"These are not toys," she told Connor, as she continued setting out a selection of swords. "Some of the crew treat them as toys. They don't get very far. We never put them to the fore in battle — they'd get minced.

"Today, I'll show you some of the main swords we use in combat. Some will feel more comfortable to you than others. Each sword has a personality. We need to find the one that fits you. It's like meeting a group of people for the first time. With some, there's an instant connection. Others, you don't click with. We need to find the right sword for you. Your sword becomes an extension of you — of your body, of your personality."

Connor nodded, fascinated.

"Bartholomew, please stand up," Cate instructed.

As he did so, she wrinkled her nose.

"What's that smell?"

"Extract of Limes," Bart said, smiling.

"Trying to ward off scurvy?" she said with a grin.

Bart puffed out his chest and grinned lopsidedly at Cate. She shook her head, all business, and threw a pair of gloves at him. He put them on and reached forward to grab the largest of the swords.

"Now, Bartholomew here, he's quite a big guy, so he carries the broadsword. It's heavy, too heavy for some, but in the right hands, it's a powerful ally."

She stepped back out of Bart's way. "A mollinet, if you please, Bartholomew."

As she moved out of his space, Bart began slicing the sword through the air. It sparkled in the sunlight. Suddenly, Bart was all business, moving with the grace of a ballet dancer, and the precision of a knife thrower, as he spun the sword left and right, up and down, circling it about his head and then to either side.

"Okay, okay, enough showing off," Cate said firmly. "Do you see, Connor, how the sword and Bart fit together?"

He nodded and high-fived Bart as his buddy set the sword carefully down on the deck and resumed his position beside him.

"Now, *you* take the broadsword. Put on these gauntlets first."

Connor stepped forward and, having slipped his hands in the rough leather gloves, reached out for the hilt of the sword. It was unbelievably heavy. It had looked as light as a reed in Bart's hands, but Connor wasn't sure if he'd even be able to hold it steady.

"That's it," Cate said, "you hold it here. We call that end part of the sword the pommel. The cross parts are the quillons. This, the tip, is the weakest part of the sword. It's called the foible."

She ran her finger along the flat edge of the sword, toward Connor's hand. "The strongest part of the blade is here. It's called the forte."

Careful to angle himself away from Cate, Connor lifted the sword, using both hands. He shivered at the power he now held in his grip. Light glinted off the edges of the blade. This was no game, Connor realized. This was an instrument of death.

"The broadsword is a cutting or hacking weapon," Cate continued, as if she had read his thoughts. "It's sharp at the end but both the sides are like razors, too. Now, let's have a look at your stance . . ."

As Cate appraised Connor's pose, he wondered how she could be so casual about the purpose of the weapon. He realized that if he was going to be a pirate, he too would have to deal with death on a daily basis. Worse than that, he would be called upon to inflict it. It was a sobering thought. Fourteen years old and a trainee assassin. He gulped.

"You want to stand a bit like a sumo wrestler, Connor, feet wider. That's it, cushion your knees. Bend them a touch more."

Connor followed Cate's instructions. She nodded approvingly. Her whole body seemed to bristle with energy.

"That's good, Connor, very good. Okay, why don't you put the sword down now?"

Gratefully, Connor set the broadsword back on the deck. He sat down again, next to Bart, full of renewed respect and admiration for his fellow pirates.

"Now, here's the thing about broadswords," Cate continued. "They're big and they're heavy. This monster's four foot long. When we board an enemy ship, time is of the essence. The broadsword's full of problems. It can get caught in the rigging, for one thing. So here's what we do. We send in Bart and a couple of the other big boys at the front. They go in and chop through the rigging, swinging their swords like windmills. It's all smoke and mirrors, though. The other crew sees these big brutes laying waste to their ship, and they're scared. But that's only setting the scene — sorry, Bart — you see, *I'm* coming in with this little baby and *I'm* the one who's going to cause the real damage."

While she was talking, Cate had picked up a smaller sword and removed it from its scabbard. It was about three-quarters of the length of the broadsword but much lighter and more delicate.

"This, my friend, is like fighting with a needle." Cate leaped forward, thrusting the sword before her.

"She's thrusting between your ribs, mate," Bart explained with a grin. "It's a quick poke that bursts your internal organs. And then it's gonna take you a day or two to die a nice slow, torturous death."

"The broadsword is all about appearance," said Cate, lunging back and forth. "The épée is about effect. In the right hands, it's poetry in motion."

Connor was starting to feel increasingly out of his depth and a little bit sick.

"You're looking a touch green, mate," Bart said. "Are you about to throw up?"

"No, no, I'll be all right." He took a few deep breaths.

"Are you sure, mate?"

Connor nodded. Cate did not acknowledge Connor's qualms. She remained focused on the job at hand, returning the épée to its scabbard and taking another of the swords in her hand.

"Now, let's try this rapier, shall we?"

She held out the sword to Connor and, taking a deep breath, he slipped his gloved hand through the handle.

"That's it. Notice the swept hilt on this sword. There we are, your whole fist goes through there. It's like a protective cage."

This felt much more comfortable than the broadsword. It was a touch shorter but significantly lighter.

"Ah, that looks good. Excellent. Now, hold the blade out flat."

Connor extended his arm.

"Good, Connor," Cate said, smiling. "Now, your hand is pronate, that means facing upward. Your stance should be soft again, your legs bent. Your weight is even between your feet. Imagine you're playing tennis. You're ready to move quickly in either direction."

Connor followed her instructions and suddenly he was having a good time. He could forget for the moment about blood and guts and death, and focus on this as just another sport. And there wasn't a sport yet that Connor Tempest had failed to master. Flushed with a new confidence, he followed Cate's flow of instructions. He could see that she was delighted with his swift progress.

"Now, we'll try a little passing forward and backward," Cate said, demonstrating the foot movements for him. "Your feet must never be together. If they are, you'll lose your balance. Just move one foot at a time, like me."

He followed her footwork, quickly picking up the rhythm. Cate stepped back and Bart joined her. Together they watched their protégé. Connor was unaware of them, lost in his determination to perfect the dancelike moves.

"Not bad for a beginner," Bart said, peeling off his gloves.

"He's an absolute natural," Cate replied. "He's exactly what we've been looking for."

Above them, standing outside his cabin, Captain Molucco Wrathe beamed with satisfaction.

"What did I tell you, Scrimshaw?" he said, stroking his

pet. "I see an exciting future ahead for Mister Connor Tempest, a most exciting future indeed."

———◆———

Connor was on a high from the sword-fighting lesson for the rest of the day. Every time he thought about it, he couldn't help but smile. Cate had said she'd give him another lesson at the same time the following morning. He couldn't wait for it.

In the meantime, there was work to be done. Connor's latest task was to clean one of the "swivel guns," or small cannons, on the foredeck. He'd been given a chamois leather and some foul-smelling polish, which he was doing his best not to inhale as he worked. It wasn't so bad when he was cleaning the top of the cannon, but now he was doing the underside and he had to lie on the deck as if he was under the body of a car. He worked as quickly as he could, anxious to get the task over with as fast as possible.

"Well, I hear you're quite the swordsman."

Connor slid forward and found Cheng Li standing there, looking down at him with a wry smile.

"I wonder," she said, "is cleaning swivel guns an appropriate job for *The Diablo*'s foremost young warrior?"

Connor scrambled to his feet, grateful for a break.

"Captain Wrathe told me we all share the jobs on board," he said, placing the lid on the can of polish.

"What a good little pirate you've become, Connor, and so quickly."

Connor was taken aback by the sarcasm in her voice. What had he done to upset her? He decided it was best to ignore it.

"Cate gave me loads of swords to try," he said enthusiastically. "I liked the rapier the best."

"Not the broadsword, like your friend Bartholomew?"

"Nah," Connor said, "too unwieldy. I want a precision weapon."

"If it's precision you're looking for, try these," Cheng Li said, lifting her arms over her head and, in a single motion, unleashing twin blades from the sheaths on her back.

"Katanas," she said, as she twisted the evil-looking blades through the air, "made to my specifications by the swordsmith on Lantao Island. A graduation gift. To myself."

The blades seemed as light as feathers, but as sharp as razors, in her hands. After a final flourish, she returned them to their sheaths. Connor was impressed.

"What about your other sword?" he asked.

"My other sword?"

He pointed to the ornate brass scabbard that hung from her waist on a leather strap.

Cheng Li looked down, suddenly pensive. She did not draw the cutlass from its sheath.

"This was my father's sword. You may have heard of him."

"Chang Ko Li," Connor said. "The best of the best, Bart told me."

Cheng Li nodded.

"The best of the best," she repeated in a surprisingly emotionless tone.

She gazed down at the scabbard, her fingers resting on the hilt of the cutlass. "They brought me this when he died. I keep it to remember."

Connor nodded. "It's good to have something to remember him by. I wish I had something of my dad's."

"You misunderstand, boy. I do not wear the cutlass to remember my father. I wear it to remember that however great you are, however far and wide they know your name, it takes only one thrust of a stranger's sword to end it all. My father, for all his reputation and glory, was killed like a common thief. *That's* the pitiable truth about the great Chang Ko Li."

With that, she removed her hand from the ancient sword. Connor could tell she was upset, though her face was steely and gave little away.

"Better get back to your cleaning," she said. "Look, warrior, you missed a spot."

22

BREAD AND SOUP

As Grace left the captain's cabin, her mind was buzzing with thoughts of Connor. When would he be joining them? Where was he now? Stepping through the door, she found herself not back on the outside deck, as expected, but in an interior corridor, lined on either side with closed doors.

The captain's cabin must have two doors, she realized. She did not dare to go back into his cabin and out through the other door. Besides, there must be another exit to the deck from this corridor.

Sure enough, as she reached the corridor's end, there was a door to her left opening out onto the deck outside. To her right, she noticed a staircase, plummeting down into the darkened depths of the ship. She should go to the left, back to the safety of her cabin or, at the very least, out onto the deserted sunlit deck.

But the stairs offered a tantalizing alternative. The captain had not forbidden her to explore the ship. He had only asked her to return to her cabin by the time the Nightfall Bell sounded. The day was still young. She had plenty of time for a quick detour to look around below-decks and get a better measure of the ship, while its inhabitants lay sleeping.

The stairs led down to another corridor. It was dimly lit with lanterns, just barely illuminating the rows of cabin doors on either side. Fortunately, a carpet — albeit a threadbare one — had been stretched out along the deck-boards and absorbed the sound of her cautious footsteps.

It was eerily silent, or maybe it just seemed that way to Grace, imagining the people, the *creatures* who inhabited the rooms around her. It was a long corridor and she was tempted to turn back again and curtail her exploration.

No, she told herself, *this is silly*. Hadn't she already met two of the vampires? For, although she had not wanted to think of them as such, that was what Lorcan and the captain were. And had they been demons? Lorcan could not have been less like one, except perhaps for that brief moment when his features had taken on a sudden harshness, but it had been so fleeting, perhaps it had only been a trick of the light.

As for the captain — of course his mask and cape were forbidding, and it took a time to grow accustomed to his strange, disembodied whisper. And yet his words had expressed only a wish to take care of her. And through the vision of Connor, he had given her hope.

The two vampires she had met had both shown her restraint and concern. Why should the rest of the crew prove any different, any more dangerous? Still, neither Lorcan nor the captain seemed keen on the thought of Grace encountering the others in an unexpected fashion. She would be wary.

Grace continued along the corridor, counting each door to try to get a better idea of the size of the crew. After twenty, she stopped counting. If there were two vampires in each cabin, that was forty already. If there were four, that was eighty. Even if each cabin was occupied by only one of them, that was still . . . something she'd prefer not to think about.

Shivering slightly, she walked on, careful to tread firmly and quietly along the center of the carpet. It reminded her of when she was young and, inspired by some movie or storybook, had gone through months determined never to step on the cracks in the pavement in case she fell through them, down into the lair of lions and tigers and bears.

At the end of the corridor was another set of stairs.

Grace hesitated, but there seemed no point in not following them down and seeing where they led — not after she had come so far.

They propelled her into another corridor, similar to the last but perhaps just a little bit narrower and strung with fewer lanterns. Was this home to more of them? It must be. Walking along, she quickly counted another thirty doors, then halted.

Again, she reminded herself that both Lorcan and the captain had promised her their protection. The captain's assurances swirled back into her head.

We're not after your blood. We have other ways to cater to the crew's needs.

What had he meant by that? she wondered, half expecting to stumble upon a hold stacked with barrels of blood — a grotesque twist on a wine cellar. The thought of it made her tremble. Perhaps it was best to return to her cabin now after all.

Just then, there was the unmistakable creak of a door opening. Grace stopped dead in her tracks. Which of the doors was it? Pressing herself into the wall, she glanced back and forth, waiting for the telltale sliver of light to reveal itself.

She held her breath as a man stumbled out from inside a cabin a few doors down from where she stood. If he turned to the right, she would be instantly discovered. She wasn't sure what would happen then but she was rea-

sonably confident it wouldn't be a happy experience —
not for her at any rate.

The man looked a little dazed and hovered outside the
open door of his cabin for a moment, unsteady on his feet.
Grace realized with a shock that it was the poor old man
she had seen at her window, fleeing Sidorio's demands.

Should she approach him? She was worried she might
scare him. Besides, what if he wasn't the poor old man he
appeared to be? What if he was a vampire, too — one
who needed blood so badly he would roam the decks to
beg for it?

She decided to follow him and watch, without making
contact. Not until she knew more about him. He seemed
in a kind of trance. Perhaps this was the depleted state the
vampires existed in during the daylight hours, weakened
even without direct exposure to the sun.

There was only so long Grace could hold her breath.
Wishing she'd attended a few more swimming classes, she
saw to her relief that the man had set off along the corridor in the other direction, reeling a little from side to side
and reaching out his hands every now and then toward
the narrow corridor's walls to steady himself.

Grace let out a quiet breath of relief, and then set off after him, very slowly and quietly, pressing herself into the
shadows and keeping a good distance between them.

He disappeared from view, but she could hear his footsteps and she imagined he must have found the stairs to

one of the other decks. Sure enough, she herself came to another flight of stairs, leading down still deeper into the ship. Beneath her, she saw his head fleetingly before he set off along the corridor below. She waited a couple of beats, then followed him.

The next corridor was different. There was no carpet here and far fewer doors. Up ahead, a door was open and bright light spilled out. The vampire quickened his pace and darted into the lit doorway. Grace scuttled after him, diving silently into the shadows behind the door.

Through the thin gap between the door and the wall, she could see that a sizable galley kitchen lay beyond. She could smell food, too. It was good. She hadn't been aware of her hunger, but the aroma was so good, it was utterly impossible to resist the heady smell. She had stepped out of the shadows and into the heart of the light. She might as well have stepped onto a spotlit theater stage. She found herself looking into the kitchen and facing a harassed-looking cook and the vampire, who seemed somewhat irritated by her appearance.

"Don't just stand there, missy," said the cook — a round, red-faced woman — "come in here and take a seat. I'll see to you in a minute, just wait your turn."

The woman turned her head as Grace obediently pulled out a stool and sat down at a counter.

"Jamie! Jamie! Where *has* that boy got to?!"

She tutted and turned back to the vampire Grace had

followed. In the bright kitchen, his skin looked as pale and fragile as tracing paper.

"You wait there, Nathaniel," the cook said. "I'll fetch you a nice bowl of soup."

Soup? Vampires didn't eat soup. Did they?

But sure enough, the cook dipped a ladle into a saucepan of bubbling liquid and transferred it into a deep bowl. She set the bowl on a tray, with a hunk of black bread, cut from a loaf fresh from the oven, and passed it to the vampire.

Vampires didn't eat bread, either — Grace was pretty sure of that.

He dipped his nose into the spiraling steam and broke into a smile.

"That'll see you right, Nathaniel," said the cook.

The vampire nodded at her and ambled out of the kitchen, carrying the tray. Grace wondered if he'd make it back to his cabin without dropping it.

"Now then, a hot bowl of broth for you, too?" The cook did not wait for an answer before dipping the ladle back into the bubbling saucepan.

"Jamie," she called over her shoulder, "Jamie, I hope you're not sleeping. There are plenty of jobs to do and I've only got the one pair of hands! Jamie!"

Grace wasn't sure whether the cook's red face came from the steam and heat of the kitchen, or from shouting so much. Wasn't she afraid she'd disturb the crew, wake them from their sleep? The sleep of the dead, Grace thought ruefully.

"There we go, dig in," said the cook, placing a bowl of soup on the counter in front of Grace and slicing off a generous chunk of bread to go with it.

Grace pulled herself closer to the counter and hungrily tucked in. The soup was delicious, though she was unsure exactly what flavor it was — certainly nothing she had ever tasted before. It was a deep pink color, but the bowl was soon clean and white and empty again.

"Well, someone was hungry!" the cook said. "Have a drop more? Yes, of course, rude not to!"

With that, she seized the bowl and filled it to the brim again.

Grace was surprised at the intensity of her own hunger. It was painful waiting for the second bowl to arrive before her. Impatiently, she tapped her foot against the stool as the cook sliced her some more bread. Grace realized that her body was crying out for food, for *this* food.

It was a wonderful relief to dip her spoon back into the bowl and capture another mouthful of the broth. She barely drew breath as she spooned every last drop of it into her mouth. The black bread was as tasty as the broth. She tore it into pieces, and used it to mop up every lingering smear of soup from the side of the bowl.

"Will you look at that, Jamie?" the cook said. "The new ones are always the worst, aren't they?"

Grace looked up curiously, her tongue wiping the last droplets of soup from the sides of her mouth. *The new ones. The new what?* She was about to ask when she felt a sudden, overwhelming sense of tiredness. The cook and the boy in front of her became a blur. As her eyes clamped shut, she felt the spoon drop from her hand. It clattered on the floor, but the sound seemed far away in the distance. She fell backward but landed, thankfully, in a waiting pair of arms. After that, she relaxed into a deep, comfortable sleep.

23

ACTION STATIONS

Connor and Bart took the second sitting of lunch. They were both ravenous after their morning's labors and tucked into mountainous portions of ocean pie, mashed sweet potatoes, and steamed seaweed. The seaweed was not only chewy, but tasted kind of nasty, and Connor pushed it to the side of his plate. "It's full of minerals," Bart told him, spooning an extra portion onto his own plate. "Great for building lean muscle." Connor tried another bite. It was like eating rubber shavings.

As Bart lit a cigarette and went to fetch them both some tea, Connor let out a yawn. It had been a long morning and he was ready for a siesta. Looking around the mess hall, he could see the other pirates were in a similar frame of mind. A few had dozed off at the table and were lying on the benches or else slumped back against their neighbor. One unlucky soul had evidently been overcome by weariness during his meal and fallen headfirst into his mashed potatoes. Connor smiled — he was tired, but he wasn't *that* tired.

Suddenly, a loud bell clanged. Connor jumped out of his seat. The bell clanged again. Pirates, who a moment ago had been snoring loudly, stirred into life and ran out of the mess hall, completely alert, swords jostling at their waists. All, that is, except the one laggard whose face was buried in his lunch.

"Come on, buddy, look lively."

Bart thrust an enamel mug, brimming with tea, into Connor's hand.

"Bring it with you," he said.

"Where are we going?" Connor asked.

"Up to the main deck," Bart cried over the din. "Captain's briefing."

"Captain's briefing?"

"You'll see. Come on, get a move on. I want a good seat."

The deck was filling up fast as Connor and Bart got there. Nevertheless, Bart managed to weave his way through the crowd and Connor followed in his wake. This was no mean feat, carrying a mug of tea, and Connor received more than one irate glance as he slopped hot tea on another pirate's jacket or over his boots. Somehow, they made it right to the front of the crowd. Connor sat down cross-legged and found himself at the feet of Captain Wrathe, who was deep in conversation with Cutlass Cate. Scrimshaw, Connor noticed, was circled around the captain's arm and appeared to be closely following Cate's words. Behind her, a large blackboard was propped on an easel and, as she talked to the captain, Cate's hand flew across the board, leaving a blur of intricate chalk marks.

Finally, the bell clanged again. Cheng Li arrived on deck, looking rather harassed.

"Why wasn't I told about this?" she snapped at Cutlass Cate, who shrugged and turned back to her blackboard.

"Captain Wrathe, I must speak with you," Cheng Li said.

But the captain was having none of it. "After the briefing, Mistress Li," Connor heard him say.

"But, Captain, I really —"

"After the briefing." There was steel in his voice.

Connor could see that relations between Captain Wrathe and his deputy were worsening every day. No wonder Cheng Li gave anyone who crossed her path a tongue-lashing. Her power on the ship appeared to be challenged at every turn. It didn't help that the pirates regarded Cutlass Cate with such natural respect and affection that anyone would think *she* was the deputy.

Captain Wrathe turned to face the expectant audience. "Okay. Is everybody here?"

"Aye, Captain," came the cry from a few of the pirates. As roll calls went, thought Connor, it was far from thorough.

"And is everybody in the mood to get filthy rich?" asked the captain.

This time, there were rather more "ayes."

"Excellent, excellent," said Captain Wrathe, his eyes sparkling as brightly as the sapphires he wore on his fingers.

"Well, my friends, word has reached us of a ship that has lately departed from Puerto Paraiso, laden — I say LADEN — with fine treasures."

Captain Wrathe's attention appeared distracted for a moment by the late arrival of one of his men.

"Sorry I'm late, Cap'n."

A gawky pirate, his face half covered in mashed potato, squeezed into the space next to Bart.

"That's all right, Young Bobby," said Captain Wrathe. "You just finish your lunch now, eh?"

There was a ricochet of laughter from the crew, but Captain Wrathe silenced it with a raise of his hand.

"As I say, this ship is heading up the coast. It seems that one of the richest dandies of Puerto Paraiso is shipping off some of his finest treasures to his summer house."

"Ooh, his summer house! That's posh!" cried one pirate.

"It is, Mister Joshua, isn't it?" answered Captain Wrathe,

clearly amused. "I say 'house,' but really it's more like a palace."

Connor was enjoying himself. He liked the way Captain Wrathe joked around with his crew. It was rather like watching a pantomime.

"Now, which of you fellows is up for a lark?" the captain asked.

"Aye, Captain."

"I'm sorry," said the captain, raising a hand to his ear, "I'm a little hard of hearing."

"AYE!" roared the pirates. Connor joined in the cry loudly. Captain Wrathe heard him and gave him a wink. Scrimshaw also appeared to look Connor right in the eye. It still unnerved him to be monitored by the snake.

"Marvelous," Captain Wrathe continued. "Well, by our calculations, the way their ship is sailing, we can catch it by teatime, board it, and be home with its booty in time for supper. You hear that, Bobby? In time for supper!"

Bobby, who was licking the mashed potato off his face, nodded enthusiastically.

"Is everybody in?" Captain Wrathe cried.

"Aye, Captain," the crowd roared once more.

But there was one voice that did not join in.

"Captain, a question."

"Yes, Mistress Li."

"Is this ship actually sailing in our sea lane? Puerto Paraiso is a way away."

"We've discussed this before, Mistress Li. I don't care for this notion of pirate captains being allocated sea lanes. If I see a ship of treasure sailing nearby, then why should I let another captain grab it?"

"Here, here!" came a hearty call from the crowd.

Cheng Li shook her head. "With the utmost respect, Captain Wrathe, there are regulations laid down by the Pirate Federation . . ."

Molucco Wrathe mimed a yawn, provoking a good deal of laughter in the crowd.

"I realize that you find this a boring topic, Captain, but — again, with utmost respect — I am the one who has to clean up the mess after we flagrantly ignore these regulations."

"I'm sorry that it affects you so."

"It affects all of us," Cheng Li said, her voice snapping. "If we enter another ship's sea lane, then we not only flout the rules of the sea, we invite attack from the pirates who we insult by trespassing into their waters."

"All right," Captain Wrathe said calmly. "All right, Mistress Li. Your point is fair. And *The Diablo* is a democracy. Let's put this to a vote. All those who feel we should let this treasure ship go, out of respect to our pirate comrades, say 'aye.'"

There was silence on the deck. Connor winced to see Cheng Li humiliated so. He could only imagine the rage she was feeling inside. He knew it would find its way out at some time and he hoped he wouldn't be close by when it did.

Captain Wrathe continued remorselessly. "Now, all those in favor of taking the treasure and taking our chances . . ."

This time, there was a deafening response. Connor felt the deckboards resound with the noise. His heart beat fast and he felt a tingle all along his spine. He looked from Captain Wrathe to Bart, who had joined in the cheers spreading like wildfire across the deck. Connor looked over his shoulder and saw the sea of pirates chanting, hands raised in support of the captain.

"I think you have your answer, Mistress Li," Captain Wrathe said.

"Yes," she said, without granting him the courtesy of the formal greeting. Connor wondered if Captain Wrathe would bring her up on this, but he let it pass.

"I do hope you will feel able to still fight with us, Mistress Li. You are one of our more brutal attackers and I have no doubt we shall want you at the heart of this raid."

"I am deputy captain of *The Diablo*," Cheng Li said icily. "Of course, I will honor my duty."

"Tickety-boo," Captain Wrathe said, "tickety-boo. And now let's have a word or two on strategy from my esteemed colleague Miss Catherine Morgan, known more commonly in these parts as Cutlass Cate."

Captain Wrathe stepped back and Cate came forward.

Two other pirates sprung from the crowd to wheel forward the blackboard.

"Okay, guys," said Cate, as businesslike as ever, a stick of blue chalk in her hand. "Today we'll be working as three teams in a 4-8-8 formation. You know the ropes . . ."

She turned to the blackboard and made crosses with the blue chalk over her initial drawing, which Connor now saw resembled a deck, seen from above.

"Our intelligence tells us the target ship is a standard galleon. After we send out the cannon fire, forward teams will enter here, here, and here. Joshua, Lukas, Bartholomew . . . you'll lead with the other broadsworders. Do your stuff. I want to see the rigging cut to pieces when the rapier bearers make the deck."

Her chalk swept over the board, circling over the crosses she'd made earlier.

"Rapier teams, you know who you are. We'll follow in tightly. Watch your forwards and keep pace with them. I don't want an inch between you, you understand. As they open up the space, you seize it. I want that crew defeated before they even realize what's going on. That's the key to bringing back the treasure. Now . . ."

Cate turned away from the blackboard to face the crew square on. Her expression was grave.

"I want minimal bloodshed. This is about booty, not body count. Some of us have been getting a little over-eager out there. Javier? De Cloux? Rein it in, boys, you understand? There's more skill in a sword that *doesn't* return with blood on its tip."

Connor was relieved, and a little surprised. After Cate's words during his sword-fighting lesson, he'd come away with the impression that blood and guts were all in a day's work for her and the rest of the crew.

"Wise words, Cate," said Captain Wrathe, stepping back into the fray. "And I hope you all listened well. It's up to you experienced pirates to set a good example for the new recruits."

The men fell silent, thinking on Cate and the captain's words.

"And now," said Captain Wrathe, smiling again, "make sure your swords are oiled and ready. Set the sails to the west and prepare yourselves for battle! Prepare for sweet riches. If you do well — and I know you shall — I can promise you a night of delight, over yonder at Ma Kettle's Tavern."

At these words, a vast whoop arose from the crowd. The pirates began dispersing as quickly as they'd arrived.

Bart stepped forward to talk to Cate. Cheng Li stormed off, saying nothing. Connor found himself facing Captain Wrathe.

"This boy needs a sword, Cate," said the captain.

He winked at Connor again, slapped Bart on the back, and strode off to ready the ship for attack.

Cate and Bart turned to Connor.

"Are you sure you're ready for this?" Cate asked.

Connor shrugged.

"He's ready," Bart said.

On his way back to his cabin, Connor came across Cheng Li, staring out to sea, looking the very picture of dejection. He hesitated. He was nervous to approach her but he felt he owed her some support. Captain Wrathe had rather cruelly humiliated her in front of the pirates, further weakening her already dwindling authority over them. Cheng Li could be arrogant and imperious but it was she, after all, who had saved Connor from death. And, although she often had a strange way of showing it, he knew that she cared about him.

"Hello," he said.

She looked up at him. In her face, he usually saw the taut mask of the warrior. Now she looked more like a young girl. Captain Wrathe had stripped her not only of her authority but of her fight — her fire.

"Well, did you enjoy the show?" she asked bitterly.

"Not really," he said, shaking his head. "Are you all right?"

"Yes," she said, looking at him curiously. "Of course I am. I'm used to Molucco Wrathe's antics, even if that was a bit more extreme than usual. It's flattering, really."

"Flattering?" Connor didn't understand.

"He must be very threatened by me, don't you think, to attempt to put me down like that. You see, my young friend, he knows that while he may have the morons among this crew cheering his every syllable, I have *real* power behind me."

"What do you mean?" Connor asked her.

"The world of piracy is changing, boy, and men like Molucco Wrathe are going to be left behind. Being a pirate is a *jolly romp* for them. People like me — people who get things done, people with connections — we're the future."

Connor was surprised to hear her talk in quite such terms, but he supposed that after Captain Wrathe's behavior, Cheng Li's allegiance had been sorely tested. Perhaps he was the only one she felt she could vent to like this.

"There's a much bigger world of piracy than what you see on this ship, boy. *The Diablo* is — forgive the expression — merely a drop in the ocean. There will come a time, and it is not so very far away, when the Molucco Wrathes of this world will be sidelined. *Then* you'll see some excitement. Then you'll see a brave new dawn of piracy."

Cheng Li appeared to have roused herself back to something of her customary feistiness. Connor was flattered that she had included him in her vision of the future. But his feelings of warmth did not last long.

"Well, I can't stand here talking to you all afternoon, boy. These katanas need oiling for the raid."

With that, she turned and strode across the deck. Cheng Li certainly had guts. Even the humiliation she'd been subjected to had not removed her drive. If anything, it had made her even stronger and more fearsome. Connor watched the twin blades jostling on her back. He remembered Cate imploring the pirates not to inflict wounds for the sake of it. Somehow, he rather doubted that Mistress Li would be paying much attention to that. Woe betide the man or woman who came into conflict with *her* today.

24

THE NIGHTFALL BELL

"Jamie, where ARE you? Jamie!"

Grace had been woken by more pleasant alarms in her time, but there was no doubting the effectiveness of the cook's shrill cries. She opened her eyes and was instantly propelled back into the steam and heat and ceaseless clatter of the galley. She was lying on the floor in the corner, a starchy tablecloth covering her as a makeshift sheet.

The cook was noisily checking pans, lifting lids and slamming them down like a drummer with a confident but erratic sense of rhythm. Jamie appeared to have disappeared again.

"Where are you, my boy? I've only got the one pair of hands, haven't I? Oh, it's just too much for a woman of my age!"

"Can I help you?" Grace asked, clambering to her feet and folding up the linen tablecloth along its deep creases.

"You?" The cook stopped dead in her tracks. "That's a little irregular. I could do with the help, but no, you need to rest and build up your strength."

Grace shook her head. "I feel great, thanks. I don't know what was in that soup, but I'm full of energy."

The cook smiled at her. "Thank you, missy, I'm glad to hear it. Very well, I shan't look a gift horse in the mouth. Just don't expect me to reveal any of my secret ingredients, eh?" She waved a spatula at Grace in a far from threatening manner.

"Absolutely," Grace said. "Now, where shall I start?"

"Well, these carrots need slicing and dicing, for starters."

Grace looked at the mountain of carrots, more than she had ever seen even at the harbor market. Undeterred, she grabbed a handful and set them down on a chopping board.

"That's very good," the cook said, watching Grace start work. "Just the right size, too. You *are* an unexpected blessing, aren't you?"

As the cook rushed over to tend to the rest of her dishes, Grace busied herself with the carrots. She'd always enjoyed the repetitive aspects of cooking — finding that it gave her a sense of calm and control, especially when such feelings were in short supply elsewhere. She was reminded of suppertime back at the lighthouse when her dad used to prepare feasts for the three of them, and she and Connor would help out with the chopping and stirring and, best of all, tasting.

"How you doing there?"

A beaming face appeared on the other side of the counter. It was not the cook but the elusive Jamie.

"I'm fine," Grace said.

"You're a quick worker," he said, throwing a slice of carrot into his mouth.

Grace shrugged. "The last thing I expected to find on this ship was a kitchen."

"Folks gotta eat, miss," said Jamie.

"Yes, *people* do, but not . . ." She lowered her voice. "But not *vampires*."

Her eyes met Jamie's.

"Oh, this grub isn't for them," he said, slipping another couple of carrot pieces into his mouth.

"Then who?" Grace asked.

"Jamie! Jamie, will you stop distracting the girl and make yourself useful. Fetch that steak out from the icebox."

"Duty calls," Jamie said, slipping away before Grace had a chance to press him for an answer to her question.

The cook came over and patted Grace's shoulder.

"That's fast work, my girl," she said. "I might have to have a word with the captain about you. Seems an awful waste when I could make use of you here in the kitchen. Could do with another pair of hands to make up for that good-for-nothing lump of a nephew of mine."

An awful waste? What was she talking about? Grace remembered the words the cook had uttered before she'd fallen asleep.

The new ones are always the worst, aren't they?

What was she talking about? A tide of panic was starting to rise. Beyond her, Jamie hauled a mound of beef out of the ice.

"What is going on here?" Grace cried, dropping her knife. "Who is all this food for?"

"Careful, missy," the cook said. "Look, you've gone and cut yourself now."

Grace looked down. Sure enough, the knife had made a neat incision into her finger and a small drop of blood was budding on her skin.

Before she knew it, the cook had grabbed her hand in a tight grip. "Quick, Jamie, move yerself. Move yerself, you lump. Oh, what a waste!"

Grace trembled but could not escape the cook's vise-like grip. As she looked up, she saw to her horror that the woman's face was changed. Her eyes were glassy and her whole expression was vacant, as if life had departed from the shell of her body and gone elsewhere. Grace thought how Lorcan's features had distorted in her cabin. This was both the same and yet different. Was the cook another vampire? What about Jamie? Grace had thought she'd be safe here, in this warm, bustling part of the ship. How little she really knew.

Jamie joined his aunt and reached out toward Grace's hand, wiping her finger clean and wrapping a small bandage neatly around it.

"That should stem the flow," he said.

Numbly, Grace looked down at her bandaged hand.

"That was close," the cook said. Suddenly all cheery business again, she released Grace's hand. "A kitchen is no place for sloppy hygiene! I'd better get these carrots over to the pan. And you, missy, had better take a break. I'm not so sure you *are* cut out for kitchen work after all. Bit too highly strung. Maybe the captain's way is best after all."

"What *is* the captain's way?" Grace asked. "Please stop talking in riddles and just tell me what's going on!"

"I must say, *you've* woken up from your sleep in a nasty little mood," the cook said, frowning.

"Just tell me," Grace repeated.

"Surely you know the score," the cook said, smiling at her with just a hint of malice. "You're the new donor, aren't you? Old Nathaniel's being retired and you're to take his place."

Donor? Grace wasn't sure what the cook meant but it didn't sound good. She wanted to ask more but, as she opened her mouth, no words came. She remembered the sight of Old Nathaniel giddily making his way to the kitchen, his skin pale and thin as if thoroughly drained of blood. What was the malevolent cook telling her? That Old Nathaniel wasn't a vampire at all? Then what?

You're the new donor.

We have other ways to cater to the crew's needs.

Things were starting to make sense. Maybe she had been wrong to place her trust in certain people. Grace found herself cold and trembling.

Then a bell began to toll.

"Is that the time? Quick, Jamie, back to work, or we'll never be ready for the Feast."

The Feast?

The bell tolled again.

"Is that the Nightfall Bell?" Grace asked Jamie.

He nodded, throwing a deep red apple in the air and catching it between his teeth. He had unusually sharp teeth, she thought, as he bit deep through the skin and into the creamy white flesh. But vampires didn't eat food, did they? This was all so confusing.

"I have to go," she said, feeling nauseous. "I have to get back."

"Ta ta, then."

Jamie smiled at her, his mouth opening up as he crunched the last of the apple down — pips, core, stem, and all.

25

RAID

Connor waited with his team for the cannon to signal the start of the attack. His heart was thudding with anticipation. Only about half of the pirates would take part in the raid. The target galleon, which they were fast gaining on, was smaller than the pirate ship, so sixty men and women were assigned to do the job.

There were three teams of twenty — each further divided into three smaller teams of four, eight, and eight. Hence the 4-8-8 formation Cate had talked of before. Connor was experienced enough at team sports to quickly grasp her strategy. It was pretty simple. The "four" was a team of four broadsworders who would go in first to scare the defending crew witless, to wield their hefty swords and do what surface damage they could to the rigging and other parts of the ship. Only surface damage. The ship was not to be significantly wrecked, on the off chance that Captain Wrathe decided to sequester it for his own use.

Once the broadsword teams had caused chaos and fear on the deck, they would be followed closely by the first teams of eightsmen. Equipped with the smaller, lethal weaponry of rapiers, épées, and daggers, the first eightsmen identified their human targets and closed in for the attack. As Cate reminded her team in her final briefing, the idea was to get the defending crew to submit and yield their cargo, *not* to kill them for sport.

The job of the teams of second eightsmen, to which one Connor Tempest had lately been drafted, was to support the first attack. The first eight had senior status and could order around their support. Each of the first eight was paired with one from the second; Connor was honored to find himself designated Cate's second.

"It's the safest position in the team," Bart told him. "Cate does enough for three men. But you'll get up close to the action, make no mistake about that. And listen to her. Do everything she asks and we'll all get home safe for the party."

Bart slipped on his leather gauntlets and shook Connor by the hand.

"Best of fortune to ya, Mister Tempest."

"And to you," said Connor.

Smiling as ever, but all business, Bart rushed off to join the other three hulks who made up his team of four.

Connor rejoined his team, who were psyching themselves up for the attack, much like the sports teams Connor had played on since he was a young kid. Some of the pirates were limbering up — lunging forward to loosen their legs or twisting from side to side to ensure they could achieve the maximum range of motion. Others were practicing stabbing and slicing through the open air with their rapiers. Thinking of the swords in real action made Connor shiver and feel somewhat nauseous.

He brushed his fingers against the hilt of the rapier that now hung at his own hip. Cate had gone through Connor's role within the attack and told him that it was highly unlikely he'd be called upon to use the sword for anything more than intimidation. But this was not a game. Nothing was guaranteed. Connor felt the weight of the sword. It was heavy, but heavier still was his growing sense of dread at using it. Maybe he wasn't cut out for the life of a pirate after all. But it was too late to step away now — the others were depending on him.

Suddenly, Cheng Li appeared at his side. He had thought for sure she'd have been one of the first eights. Perhaps she was just coming to wish him luck.

"I'm joining this team," Cheng Li announced. "Johnna — go and take my place in the first eights. You've been promoted. I'm staying back to keep my eye on Tempest."

The other pirate — Johnna — was clearly delighted. She saluted Cheng Li then raced over to join the rest of her team. Connor looked at Cheng Li. Had she actually chosen to step back, he wondered, or had she been demoted? Her dark eyes warned him not to even think about it further.

Suddenly, there was a deafening noise from right above Connor's head. Looking up, he saw a heavy metal grid falling toward him. Instinctively, he jumped out of the way. As he did so, the narrow grid swung down but came to a halt at a forty-five-degree angle. Two similar structures had appeared at intervals farther along the deck. They jutted out menacingly like half-raised drawbridges.

"What are those?" Connor asked Cheng Li, already suspecting the worst.

"How do you think you're going to get over from our ship to theirs?" she replied.

Connor looked up at the narrow grid that hovered above his head, as the ship rocked from side to side. It looked far from stable.

"When the cannon sounds," Cheng Li told him, "it will swing down until it's flat and make a bridge."

Connor was unconvinced.

The pirate on his other side nudged him. "We calls 'em the 'Three Wishes,'" he said, "cuz all you can do is wish that you make it over to the other ship and safe home again."

"Thanks," said Cheng Li testily, "that's *very* helpful."

Connor felt really sick.

The cannon sounded.

The pirate ship had drawn up alongside its target, easily outrunning the smaller craft, like a shark closing in on a dolphin.

The vessels clashed.

The noise in Connor's ears was deafening as the cannons sounded again and, at the same time, the Three Wishes were lowered to a ninety-degree angle and positioned to make bridges from *The Diablo* to the other vessel.

As the metal grids clattered into place, the three teams of broadsworders lost no time in racing over the fragile structures, high over the churning sea. Connor saw that each bridge had a thin guardrail on either side, but even so they looked anything but sturdy, lurching up and down as the two ships rocked in the rough water.

"I can't do it," Connor said, panic spreading through him like ice.

"Of course you can," Cheng Li said. "The trick is to run over as quickly as you can. The slower you go, the more unstable you'll feel. And whatever you do, Connor, don't look down!"

But Connor couldn't help but look down right now. Far below the metal grids lay the churning ocean, waiting hungrily to receive him back into its cold embrace.

He trembled. He'd never been keen on heights — even

living in a lighthouse hadn't conquered that. He felt a heavy sickness and a frightening swell of adrenaline in his veins. One moment, his whole body felt as heavy as lead, the next as fragile and vulnerable as a feather. There was no way he could set foot on the bridge. One slip or missed footing and he'd plummet into the icy depths. He wanted to crawl away and take shelter. Why had Captain Wrathe chosen him to take part in the raid? He couldn't do this.

"Yes, you can."

It was his dad's voice once more. Right inside his head.

"You can do this, Connor."

The calmness and certainty in his dad's voice reassured him. The flow of adrenaline slowed and Connor felt a momentary calm.

"First eights in," cried Cate, suddenly breaking from the pack and darting over the wish.

And now three teams of eight pirates ran off across the metal bridges like racehorses, jumping from one ship to the other, running down their prey.

Now Connor and the others on the second team of eightsmen stepped up, in a line, to the ship's side. He was last but one. Cheng Li stood behind him.

This was it. The moment. He couldn't tell how the battle was going. It was impossible to see what was happening on the deck of the other ship.

In front of him, the wish rocked up and down. Though

he'd now seen twelve pirates safely run across it, he still feared the worst. But what option did he have now? He was part of a team and Connor Tempest never let down his team.

"Second eights," came a cry.

The pirates in front of him shot across the wish, their hands not even reaching for the guardwire. Suddenly, Connor was at the front. He hesitated for an instant, but Cheng Li gave him a firm push forward.

"Do it, boy. Prove to me I didn't rescue a coward."

Taking a deep breath, Connor jumped up onto the wish and, not looking down, not reaching out his hand, propelled himself forward. Just a few steps and he landed with a thud on the wooden deck of the vessel. He'd made it.

"Excellent, boy!" cried Cheng Li as she jumped down beside him. There was no time for further chat. Connor parted company with Cheng Li. His job was to seek out Cate and follow her instructions.

Around him, the first eights were engaged in one-on-one combat. He was so full of adrenaline, he might have been tempted to join in, but Cate's instructions had been crystal clear. There was a system and it must be kept to. Ahead, he saw Cate, signaling him over. He ran to her side. Cate's rapier was held over two men, whose faces told of surrender even if their bodies had not trembled like reeds in the wind.

"Hold them here, while I go deeper," Cate instructed.

Connor drew his own rapier and extended it toward the men, hoping that they could not sense his inexperience. Judging by their whimpering, they did not.

"Don't mess with Tempest," Cate told them. "He's one of our most bloodthirsty." Winking secretly at Connor, she moved on.

Maybe it *wasn't* so hard being a pirate, after all. Connor let out a deep breath and smiled at his captives. This seemed to unnerve them utterly.

"Just being friendly," he shrugged, cheekily moving the tip of his rapier closer to the pair.

He felt a tap on his back. He spun around. One of the defending crew had broken free and was hovering before him — a rapier in his hand. He must have taken it from one of *The Diablo*'s crew. He wore no protection, but his eyes were full of hatred.

"Bloody pirates," he said. "Think we're easy prey, do you? Well, think again."

He struck out at Connor with the sword but Connor saw the move coming and darted out of the way.

The man came right back at him, and this time the rapier grazed his shoulder. Connor felt a searing pain. But it was okay — it was better than okay. The pain was like a wake-up call. It pulled Connor together. Now they stood opposite each other, weighing the possibilities. Connor brought himself to focus, summoning up the lessons he'd learned from Cate and Bart.

"You're just a boy," sneered his opponent. "Are they running out of proper pirates and taking on youth trainees?"

He mustn't rise to the bait. The man was trying to throw him off his guard. Connor kept his gaze fixed on the man's eyes. It paid off. As the man took another swing at him, Connor predicted the move and blocked the blade with his own. Then he used all his strength to force down the attacking rapier. As he did so, pain shot through his shoulder. The effort had been too much. He could feel warm blood seeping from the wound.

He mustn't let himself get distracted. He'd have to get in the next attack first. And he did. He pulled his rapier away and dived toward his opponent, roaring with adrenaline. His eyes boring into the man, he plunged his rapier toward his chest. But the deck had become wet with dirt and blood and Connor slipped. The rapier did not make the man's chest, but the attack threw him backward and his head bashed against the mast. He slumped to the floor, blood instantly gushing down over his head and face like a waterfall.

Connor's heart was racing as he reached down and tore the rapier out of the man's limp hands. When he brought his hand away, it was soaked in the man's blood. He wiped it dry on his trousers.

He didn't want the man to die. He wanted to protect

himself but he didn't want the man to die. He looked around the deck. The battle was ending. The pirates of *The Diablo* had won. But Connor didn't feel like a winner.

He raced over to the two prisoners Cate had asked him to watch over before. They had seen his duel and reared back in fright as he returned.

"Be merciful!" one of them cried.

"Take off your scarf," Connor rasped. "Take off your scarf. NOW!"

The man's shaking hands unraveled the scarf.

"Come with me!" Connor commanded him.

"Please — be merciful!"

"Just come." Connor was almost out of voice now.

He grabbed the man by the wrists and pulled him over to the mast, where his erstwhile opponent was now covered in blood from his head wound. Taking the scarf, Connor pressed it to the man's skull, holding it there to still the flow of blood.

"Here, you take over," he said, placing the other man's hand over the blood-soaked scarf. "Keep it there and keep the pressure strong. It's a bad wound but it won't be fatal."

"You are merciful! Thank you!" the man said, smiling through chattering teeth.

Connor stood there, breathing in quick bursts. He felt a hand on his shoulder. He couldn't fight anymore. There was no fight left in him.

He turned.

"Good work, boy," said Cheng Li. "We may need to work on your killer instincts, but good work all the same."

Cate came running over.

"Connor, I heard what happened. Well done! Brilliant stuff. And Cheng Li . . ."

"Yes?"

Cheng Li and Cate faced each other, their swords in their hands.

"Fantastic work, Mistress Li. As usual. Thanks for looking after Connor. But I want you back at the front of the attack next time. You put the other eights to shame. Beautiful precision wounds. You'll have to show me some of those moves with the katanas sometime."

"If you wish," Cheng Li said nonchalantly, but Connor could see that she was pleased.

Cate ran off to make official news of the ship's surrender. *The Diablo* fired two cannon shots to signal victory and the defeated ship sounded the solo cannon of surrender. And so it was over, as swiftly as it had begun.

The captain of the defeated ship had taken little convincing. He knew he was outnumbered. As Cate led him from his cabin, all he could do was moan about what his boss would say when he learned that his precious cargo had been taken.

"You can tell him that Captain Molucco Wrathe of *The Diablo* sends him his warmest regards," said a familiar voice.

Captain Wrathe stepped out from the trailing cannon smoke, looking utterly pristine, his swords already back in their silver scabbards.

"We thank you kindly for your cargo," Captain Wrathe said. "And if you'll just assist with carrying it up here for loading, we shall not impose any further upon your precious time."

On Cate's orders, Connor followed a pair of prisoners down to the hold, and kept his sword trained on them as they made four journeys each to haul up the treasures stowed below. They were too terrified to be indignant.

Finally, the bounty was piled high on the deck like a bonfire of riches. The pirates divided up again into two teams. The first eights held the defeated crew in a circle while the broadsworders and the second eightsmen collected the goods and carried them across the Three Wishes to the deck of *The Diablo*. After a couple of journeys back and forth, Connor had all but lost his earlier fear.

"Can ya give me a hand here, buddy?" Bart called.

Beaming, Connor picked up the other end of the last chest and, together, they hauled it over the wish.

The rest of the attack teams returned, jumping down from the Three Wishes triumphantly onto the deck. The three temporary bridges were raised behind them like drawbridges, dormant until the next raid.

Cheers greeted the attackers' return and there was a ceaseless round of hugs and backslapping and high fives.

"Well done, buddy!" said Bart, slapping Connor heartily on the back.

"Well done, indeed!" cried Captain Wrathe. "A fine raid, my fellows. A fine raid." He put a broad arm around Cate and hugged her. "Magnificent work, Cate, truly magnificent."

Cate blushed furiously.

"We did it," Connor said to Bart. "We did it!"

"You're a pirate now," Bart said to him. "May God help ya, you're a bona fide pirate."

Connor turned his gaze toward the ocean and saw the defeated ship beating a swift retreat toward the darkening horizon. He walked away from the others, up to the guardrail.

"I told you you could do it," said another familiar voice.

"Dad!" he said aloud.

"You did well today, Connor."

"Where's Grace?" Connor asked. "Is she alive? Where is she?"

He waited but there was silence. Behind him, he heard the jubilant crew. Why had his dad ignored his last question?

There was more cannon fire. Still he stood at the guardrail, his eyes fixed on the horizon, waiting.

At last, the calm voice spoke once more inside his head.

"Not yet, Connor. Not yet. But soon."

26

THE FIGUREHEAD

Grace turned on her feet and ran back out of the kitchen, into the corridor. Where were the stairs? How much time did she have?

The bell tolled again.

How could she have lost track of the day like this? She must have slept for far longer than she had realized. She wondered what secret ingredient the cook might have slipped into her bread and soup.

By the next toll of the bell, she had reached the corridor where Old Nathaniel had stumbled out of his cabin. It was quiet now and the doors were all closed. Perhaps there was still time.

Throwing herself at the stairway, she took two steps at a time, no longer concerned at the noise she was making.

Her heart pounded wildly. She had to make it back to her cabin before the crew awoke.

Again the bell tolled. How many strikes did she have?

Now she was in the corridor beneath the main deck. She could hear signs of life behind the closed doors. No, more like signs of *death*. *Don't even think about it, Grace, just run!*

She was already out of breath when she reached the last stairwell. If only she was as fit as Connor. *Never mind, not much farther now.* She could almost hear him giving her encouragement.

Reaching the top of the stairs, she looked back along the corridor. Then she realized there was a quicker way. The door here — the one she'd ignored earlier — opened out onto the deck. She could get to her cabin quicker that way. She pushed it open as the bell sounded once more.

It was a shock to find it was dark outside, though of course she knew it must be. But it was utterly dark and she had to pause to get her bearings. If she ran off wildly now, she might easily slip off the edge of the ship or run into the mast or some other hidden danger.

Suddenly, a glow of light appeared at her side. Gratefully, Grace looked around. The light grew stronger, strong enough to tell her that she needed to run to her left.

"Ain't you gonna stop and say how-do?"

It was a girl's voice. Behind her. Grace knew she should just put her head down and run. The captain had told her to return to her cabin by nightfall. And she'd almost made it.

"Well, that's just rude if you ask me. And I have no truck with rude persons."

"I'm sorry." Grace turned around. Better to say a quick hello and then run.

Facing her was a young woman, her hair styled in a neat bob, wearing an old-fashioned dress. There was a name for it. Grace searched her memory. A *flapper* dress, yes, that was it. She had a headband, too, with a black feather in it. And everything — the clothes, the hairband, the girl's bare feet — was all dripping wet. Her face was a mess. She'd clearly been wearing quite a bit of makeup and it was running all over the place, making her eyes swim in pools of black and her small bow-shaped mouth drip with scarlet.

"It's rude to stare, don't you know?" the girl said. "Even if I *am* quite beautiful."

"I'm sorry," Grace said. "I was just thinking . . . how pretty your dress is."

It wasn't at all what she had been thinking but it turned out to be just the right thing to say. The girl's lips parted in a broad smile.

"Why, thank you. It's an original copy of a Chanel, don't you know. I'll be changing in a moment, once I've finished my nightfall duties."

The girl waved a lit taper, raising it to a lantern, which

blossomed into light. Carefully, she closed the lantern again and walked, with the elegance of a ballet dancer, to the next one, just at Grace's side.

"Are you Miss Flotsam?" Grace asked, suddenly putting the pieces together.

"Why, yes," she said, smiling prettily again. "Darcy Flotsam, entertainer at large, formerly of *The Titania*. And who might you be?"

"Grace, Grace Tempest."

"Charmed, I'm sure," said Miss Flotsam, pausing in her duties to give Grace a little curtsy.

What a strange doll-like creature she was, thought Grace.

"So you rang the bell," Grace said.

"That is correct. I always ring the bell. I'm always the first one up. It's my duty to sound the bell and then to light the lanterns. And then I can go and get changed out of these wet things into something lovely and dry."

She continued past Grace, opening up the next lantern. Grace should really be getting back inside, but her cabin was close now. And the deck was still deserted, save for the two of them. No harm could come from talking a while longer to Darcy Flotsam, surely.

"How did you get so wet?" Grace asked.

Miss Flotsam giggled. "Silly, I took a little swim, of course, like I always do. It's important to have a good stretch at the end of the day, especially when you have a" — she took a deep breath — "sed-en-ta-ry job like mine."

"A sedentary job?"

"*Characterized by much stillness and little physical exercise* . . . Mr. Byron taught me that. He's very good with words."

"What exactly *is* your job?" Grace asked.

Miss Flotsam turned and adopted a balletic posture, raising her whole body in a fine arch. She reached her arms back behind her waist and set her face forward, nose tilted to the sky.

"There's your clue," she said.

Grace shook her head, utterly confused.

"Why, I'm the ship's figurehead, aren't I?"

Grace looked over to the prow of the ship and noticed that there was indeed now an empty space where the figurehead had been. Could this really be true? On this ship, anything was possible.

"Figurehead by day, figure of fun by night," Miss Flotsam said. "Trust me, dearie, if you had to hold that position for fourteen hours at a stretch, you'd need a good old swim at the end of it, too!"

"But how?"

"Oh, it's a long and fascinating story," said Miss Flotsam, closing the lamp as she spoke and stepping elegantly on to the next. "I was an entertainer, a *chanteuse,* on the great cruise ship, *The Titania*. I sang after second supper each night and all the posh gents and ladies, they loved my singing and my little dances. Well, you'll remember, I'm sure, what occurred that fateful night when *The Titania* was struck mid-ocean by a powerful bolt of lightning. We sank. We were all thrown in the water, but something curious happened to me. We'd sunk on the very site where an old galleon had been wrecked. I knew nothing of this till much later, of course. I was sleeping, you see . . . I had crossed. But later, when they salvaged the wrecks, they found this beautiful figurehead lying on the ocean floor . . . me! For, somehow, I had become one with the galleon's figurehead. So they salvaged me and took me away to a very important nautical museum. They gave me a special tag and put me in the storeroom for safekeeping while they decided where best to display me. I lay there for several days and nights, and then I got bored. And, one night, I just opened my eyes, stretched my legs, climbed up from the bench, and walked out of the very important nautical museum . . ."

"So you're a vampire, too," Grace said, her eyes wide with wonder.

"I am *not* a vampire." Miss Flotsam shook her head firmly, her neat bobbed hair spinning over her cheeks. "I'll have you know, I'm a Vam-pi-rate."

Grace couldn't help but smile.

"So, what's *your* story, Grace?" Miss Flotsam asked her.

"Yeah, what *is* your story?"

It wasn't Miss Flotsam who spoke. This was a gruff male voice. They were no longer alone. Grace had chatted for too long, allowing herself to become distracted.

Miss Flotsam quivered. "Good evening, Lieutenant Sidorio."

"Hey, Darcy. Well, aren't you going to introduce me to your friend?"

Grace took a breath and turned. Facing her was a tall, bald-headed man, his muscles seeming to burst from clothes that were a cross between those of a sailor and a gladiator. She recognized him, but he didn't seem to remember her.

"Grace Tempest, may I introduce you to Lieutenant Sidorio," said Miss Flotsam. "Lieutenant Sidorio, may I —"

"Yeah, yeah," he said, in a voice like crunching gravel, "we get the picture, Darcy. So, Grace, huh? When did you rock up on board? And are you a vamp or a donor?"

There it was again. That awful word. *Donor*.

Grace thought of Old Nathaniel and his blood-drained pallor.

You're the new donor . . .

You're to take his place . . .

And suddenly, Grace knew she was trapped.

27

THE SLOW PARADE

"Well," said Sidorio, staring hard at Grace, "which is it? Vampire or donor?"

Still speechless, Grace looked at him. It was like facing a wall of muscle. His neck was as thick as the trunk of a well-established tree. His arms were far broader than her own legs.

"Great," he said dismissively, "just what we need, another dumb one."

Grace was enraged, but still said nothing. The last thing she wanted was to anger him.

"Sidorio! Hey, Sidorio!" came a call from behind Grace.

Sidorio looked over Grace's head. As he did so, he opened his mouth and idly began picking at something between his teeth. Looking up, Grace saw that he had two oversized canine teeth, apparently made of gold. They would bore into you like a knife through butter, she thought. It made her blood run cold.

"I've been looking all over for you, Lieutenant," said Lorcan, slipping briskly past Grace, as if he hadn't seen her. "I need to talk to you, urgently. Captain's business."

"Sure," Sidorio said, seeming in no rush. He dipped his head in Grace's direction. "You seen the latest addition to the crew?"

Lorcan turned. "Oh, yes. Grace," he said matter-of-factly. "Sorry, I didn't see you there."

"You know her?"

"Yes, yes," said Lorcan, who appeared to have something far more important to discuss. "I'm the one who fished her out of the water."

Sidorio seemed to have lost interest.

"I've got news, Lorcan," Grace began, enormously relieved to see her friend.

"That'll be Midshipman Furey to you," Sidorio said.

Lorcan did not even attempt to defend her but surveyed Grace with the same cold eyes as Sidorio, then turned his back on her altogether.

Grace felt as though she'd been punched. Why was Lorcan acting this way with her? She had thought he was her friend. He'd been so kind to her before.

"I really do have to talk to you, Sidorio," Lorcan continued. "Alone."

He extended a hand toward Sidorio's rippling forearms and pulled him away from the others.

Grace felt utterly deflated at being ignored and talked over, but when the men had moved a short distance away, Lorcan turned back to her, his blue eyes full of concern. He made a pointing gesture with his finger. Grace realized he was telling her to go back to her cabin.

Well, maybe she would, and maybe she wouldn't. Maybe it was time for Grace to call the shots.

Miss Flotsam nudged Grace. "He was just playing tough to impress Lieutenant Sidorio. Typical man!"

Grace smiled weakly, at least a little relieved at the thought.

"I think you're a bit sweet on Midshipman Furey," said Miss Flotsam. "And who could blame you? He's a definite looker. That hair. Those eyes."

Grace found herself blushing as Miss Flotsam continued.

"Course he's not right for me. I'm saving myself for Mister Jetsam, my one true love."

She sighed at the thought. "Well, I must get on and finish lighting the lamps. I can't just stand here, conversing with the likes of you all evening." She smiled. "But I'll see you later, Grace. And I'll lend you a nice dress, too. You'll want to look your best for the Feast."

With a wink, she continued on her way, taper in hand.

The Feast? Grace remembered that there had been talk of a feast when she'd first arrived on the ship. But what exactly *was* the Feast? Was it to be tonight? Was that why the cook and her boy had been so frantic in the galley?

Jamie had told her that the plentiful food was not for the vampires. Of course not. It was for the donors. So maybe the Feast was simply a great feast for the donors. And, like the cook, Miss Flotsam had simply assumed that she was a donor.

The more she thought about it, the more she realized she *must* be a donor. She certainly wasn't a vampire and, according to Sidorio, you were either one thing or the other. She still hadn't gotten to the bottom of what the donors did. The most obvious answer was that they gave their blood to the vampires. And yet, the captain had said that they didn't want her blood. Her mind was circling back on itself. She needed to speak to Lorcan. She'd learned a lot since she'd last quizzed him about the ship. Now she had some specific questions, which needed his answers.

He had told her to go back to her cabin and that seemed like the best idea. They could talk privately there and there would be no distractions. She made her way along the deck, careful to stick to the shadows and not draw further attention to herself. A flock of vampires was gathering on deck, though they seemed far too engrossed in their own conversations to notice her.

They were fascinating to observe — a real jumble of people, nothing like the images of vampires Grace had grown up with. There were those, like Darcy Flotsam, who had clearly kept the fashion of the era in which they had "crossed." Others, like Sidorio, wore a blend of attire, which made it harder to place them in time or space. Many, like Lorcan, seemed to have adopted the universal costume of a pirate or seafarer. And still others looked like nothing and no one Grace had seen before — impossibly glamorous and otherworldly. As Grace watched the strange parade languidly pass by, she thought how their apparent age gave little indication of how old they truly were. How did they measure age? she wondered. Was it from their actual birth? Or from the time they "crossed"? And what tales did they have of their crossing? If they were as intriguing as Miss Flotsam's, Grace was keen to hear them. Perhaps that might be her role aboard the ship, Grace thought, remembering the pencils and notebooks in her cabin. She could be the ship's chronicler. That would keep her busy, more than busy, until she found Connor again. She had to keep focused on that and not let the strangeness of the ship distract her at every turn. She had to talk to the captain again and persuade him to help her — to stop every passing ship if that was what it took.

Although she was close to her cabin now, she paused in the shadows, not yet ready to leave her first sight of the ship's inhabitants.

From the safety of the shadows, Grace watched and listened as they passed. Much of their words seemed merely pleasantries — the kind of social chit chat that was common in the harbor, though it sounded a little more formal here.

"Good evening to you, madam. I trust you passed a peaceful sleep."

"I did, sir. And yourself? Good. Of course, I always feel a little more tired at this time of the week."

"Yes, I know what you mean. I could barely raise myself from my bed tonight but then I remembered that it was Feast night."

"Quite, quite. By the time the Dawning Bell sounds, we shall all be reborn."

"Yes, indeed. Bring on the donors, say I, and not a moment too soon!"

This latest mention of the donors was enough to propel Grace, at last, toward her cabin. As she opened the door, she found Lorcan already waiting for her, a book in his hand. Had she really kept him waiting so long?

As she closed the door behind her, he looked up and shut the book, too.

"Tell me about the Feast," she said.

Unsurprised, he nodded and indicated that she should pull up a chair.

28

THE DIVIDING OF THE SPOILS

The deck of *The Diablo* was crowded once more. And this time, it was not just full of people. The returning pirates had spread out the booty they'd taken across the Three Wishes. It had been a good haul. There were heavy oak chests, their gaping mouths dribbling purses of gold onto the deck. There was fine jewelry, paintings and sculptures, ornate clocks, antique urns, gilded mirrors, crystal chandeliers, and all manner of fine things. The foredeck, Connor thought, resembled a street market — but one where the merchandise was unbelievably rare and precious and where you could be confident that nothing was fake.

In front of the booty, like a jocular street trader, stood Captain Wrathe.

The whole crew of *The Diablo* was gathered on the deck. The sixty pirates who had participated in the attack were at the front. Connor looked at his fellows. They were sweaty and grubby from their efforts, but exhilarated. They'd all been given flagons of water on their return. Connor had quickly drained his dry. Others, who had better paced themselves, were still drinking. A few poured the water over their heads to cool off and clean up at the same time.

Captain Wrathe addressed his crew. "Well, my fellows, that was a cheeky victory, was it not? Well done, well done indeed. Let's have three cheers for our military mastermind, Cutlass Cate!"

He pulled Cate out from the crowd and Connor was amused to see how she blushed as the pirates cheered for her. He joined in, loudly, as did Bart, who couldn't resist throwing in an extra whoop.

"Today we saw a fine piece of teamwork," continued Captain Wrathe. "All of you played your part and I thank you all. But I want to pay particular tribute to one brave young lad who fearlessly took part in his first raid today."

Captain Wrathe scanned the crowd for Connor.

"Where are you, Mister Connor Tempest? Come up here."

In the middle of the crowd, Connor stood frozen to the spot until a firm hand propelled him forward.

"Go on, buddy, up you go."

Then the rows of pirates ahead of him opened up to make way for him. The other pirates squeezed his shoulders and slapped him on the back as he walked forward.

"Here's the very fellow," Captain Wrathe said. "Fourteen years old and a prodigy, nothing less than a PRODIGY!"

The captain set his hand on Connor's shoulder. Now all eyes were upon him and Connor could feel himself blushing furiously.

"Let's have three cheers for Mister Tempest, boys. Hip hip . . ."

"Hooray!" cried the crew.

Connor looked out at the sea of faces as they continued their cheers. It was an incredible feeling. He belonged.

As the final cheer came, Connor felt a sudden sadness. He wished his dad and Grace could have seen him at this moment. He and Grace had always been outsiders in Crescent Moon Bay. No one but their dad had ever cheered for either of them. In spite of his considerable talents at sports, he'd never felt welcomed into a team. The other kids viewed him with suspicion as the misfit son of the reclusive lighthouse keeper.

At last, he was part of a team. He looked at Cate and Bart, both of whom grinned proudly at him and cheered. Even Cheng Li clapped and nodded. He realized that they were not just his crewmates. They were becoming his friends.

"Well, now," Captain Wrathe said, as Connor stepped

back to the ranks. "Our ship is pointed in the direction of Ma Kettle's Tavern . . ."

The cheering that followed this announcement was long and loud.

"But before we throw ourselves upon the mercies of that merry lady and her kegs, we have business to attend to. We must divide up these spoils, must we not?"

Connor fully expected Captain Wrathe to pick first, but the captain insisted that Cate step up ahead of him. Connor could see from Cate's expression that this was unexpected and an honor.

Cate briefly surveyed the vast array of items set out across the deck. Would she choose a fine set of jewels? Perhaps an ornate mirror? Or a painting of Old London, before the flood?

Cate stepped over all of these items and selected a simple bag of coins.

"Is that your best choice?" Captain Wrathe asked.

Cate nodded.

The captain did not try to dissuade her. He clearly respected Cate and the fact that she knew her own mind.

Rubbing his hands, Captain Wrathe stepped forward and appraised first one treasure then another. Now he seemed like a confident buyer, checking out the goods before entering confidently into negotiation with a trader. But there was no trader here and no need to negotiate.

The captain could choose whatever he wanted. The pirates clearly enjoyed this part of the ritual.

"Look there, Captain. That's a wondrous painting."

"No, I'd take the whale carving, if I were you."

"That's a fine clock to set your time by!"

After lengthy deliberation, Molucco Wrathe reached down and plucked a large blue sapphire from a chest of gems. As he held it aloft, there were roars of approval from the crowd. Connor had a feeling that the captain had never been in any doubt as to what he would select.

There was cheering, then hushed anticipation as the next man came up to make his selection. And so the ceremony continued as each pirate in turn was invited up to survey the booty and take his pick from the treasures there. The whole process seemed as organized a ritual as the attack itself.

Connor wondered how these practices had evolved. It was curious to think that a few days ago, he'd known nothing of this world. He'd overheard tales of pirate ships on the quayside and sometimes thought that he'd seen them from the lighthouse window. But now here he was — not just in their world, but part of it.

But while he was starting to understand the pirates' way of life, he wasn't yet comfortable with all aspects of it. He could not forget that the treasures spread out before him had belonged to a wealthy man and his family. Was being wealthy in itself a crime? And was *not* being wealthy sufficient excuse for seizing another person's property? Connor's feelings were further complicated by the sense that Captain Wrathe himself appeared anything but poor. As Connor watched each pirate in turn carry away his treasure to a storage container on the lower decks, he had cause to wonder quite how poor even the most seemingly humble of the crew might be.

"Come on, Mister Tempest, come and have a rummage."

At Captain Wrathe's bidding, the pirates around Connor stepped aside to let him through.

Reluctantly, Connor approached the spread of possessions. He surveyed the haul, casting his eyes across the clocks and mirrors and jewels. His eyes came to rest on a pile of books. Instantly, they made them think of his home in the lighthouse. His dad's most treasured possessions had been his books. They had filled every shelf in every room, sometimes double-stacked and creeping up in stacks from the floorboards, too. Connor had never been much of a reader himself but he missed seeing those books around him every day. Maybe if he took just one of these books, it would bring him back a piece of his dad.

He crouched down and lifted one of the volumes. It was a copy of *Peter Pan*. An old one with fine illustrations — not unlike the copy his dad had read to him and Grace. Connor flipped through the well-thumbed pages. The book came open at the front. There was an inscription.

To my darling son,
on his seventh birthday.
With all my love, Dad.

Connor closed the book. It had been a gift from another father to his beloved son. It wouldn't bring Connor's dad back. Nothing could do that.

Suddenly, Connor felt floods of anger that this book had been taken from the child it belonged to. Anger that he and Grace had been forced to leave Crescent Moon Bay without their dad's possessions. Anger that their dad had been taken away from them. And Grace, too. This was too much, too hard. He could play at being a man — a pirate — but he was only a boy and he wanted to go home. Only there was no longer any home for him to return to.

"What's the matter, Mister Tempest?" called Molucco Wrathe. "Can't find anything to tempt you?"

Connor shook his head. Tears were pricking his eyes but he didn't want Captain Wrathe or the rest of the crew to see him crying. He pushed through the crowd, desperate to get away.

No one took much notice and the men were grateful to move forward an inch to gain a better sight of the goods. Finally, Connor broke free of the swarm of pirates and climbed up to the upper deck. He found a perch there, right at the prow of the ship. Beneath him, the pirates swarmed over the stolen treasures, looking more predatory than ever. Connor lifted his eyes from them and out over the darkening sky and sea.

The beauty and peace of the scene made him lonely once more for the company of Grace. His dad had said she was coming back but it was hard holding on to that belief. How could he be sure he could trust that voice? Was it really that of his dead father, reaching out to him across time and space, or had he somehow conjured it up himself? As Captain Wrathe had suggested to him once before, had he confused what he felt with what he wanted to feel?

Suddenly, Connor felt an outpouring of grief for Grace. All the emotions he had somehow kept tightly controlled now bubbled up furiously inside him. All was still and silent around him. But inside, his mind was turmoil and his stomach tied itself into a thousand angry knots. Was this a sign that Grace was dead? Was she letting go? What had happened? Had the Vampirates killed her? His thoughts and fears began spinning out of control.

There had always been one surefire way to calm himself down. Connor closed his eyes and began to chant . . .

I'll tell you a tale of –

He broke off and opened his eyes again. The old shanty no longer brought him any comfort. It only made him *more* anxious about Grace.

Connor turned his eyes up to the star-filled sky. His thoughts settled upon the soothing memory of nights in the lamp room at the top of the lighthouse. Nights when the harbor was quiet and Dexter Tempest had settled his young twins on either side of him and taught them the names of the different stars and constellations. As Connor lifted his eyes to the heavens, he remembered how he and Grace had taken turns identifying them. He could hear their childish voices, chanting the exotic names.

Aquarius.

Aquila.

Carina.

Centaurus.

Corona Borealis.

Dorado.

Eridanus.

Lupus . . .

"Here he is!"

Connor's reverie was interrupted as Bart and Cate sat down on either side of him.

"We were worried about you," Bart said.

"I just needed some time to myself," Connor said.

Cate nodded. "You've had quite a day. And you've been through so much."

Though she had always been nice to him, this was the first time that Cate had really let down her guard.

"Here, buddy," said Bart, "the captain let us pick for ya."

Bart opened his palm and dropped a silver locket into Connor's hands.

"A locket?" Connor said, smiling and looking askance at Bart. "Is this a joke?"

"It's not for you, mate," Bart said, completely serious. "It's for yer sister. For when you see her again."

Connor was too touched to speak. He closed his eyes and gripped the locket tightly.

"Yeah, well," Bart mumbled. "It wasn't just my idea. Cate and I thought . . ."

His words hung in the still air.

"We think it's far too soon to give up hope," Cate said, coming to Bart's rescue.

Connor nodded, feeling the tears starting to recede. "I won't give up hope. I'll never give up hope." He unclasped the chain, slipped the locket around his own neck, and fastened it again.

"Does that look weird?" he asked.

"No, mate, it's working for me."

"Not *at all* girlie," Cate added, with a friendly shake of the head.

"Best keep it hidden at the tavern, though," Bart said. "There are wicked eyes and loose fingers aplenty at that place and they'd kill for a nice trinket like that."

Connor pushed the locket under his shirt. The metal felt cool and soothing against his heart. It seemed just the right place for it.

"What is Ma Kettle's Tavern anyhow?" he asked the others. "Everyone seems very excited about it, but I don't know what to expect."

"That's easy," Bart said. "The only thing you can safely rely on at Ma Kettle's is to expect the unexpected! It's the place where every pirate crew in this region lets off steam, with good booze and bad company. Look there, buddy, we're not far away now."

Connor followed Bart's gaze. It was true. Out of the dark velvet of the sky, the shape of the coastline was coming into focus. A rocky outcrop, like a jagged piece of coal, loomed in the distance. Out of its darkness flashed a neon light, faint and small at first, but growing larger and stronger as the ship picked up speed.

"That's Ma Kettle's," Bart announced. "Best prepare yourself, buddy. You're in for a night to remember."

Instinctively, Connor reached his arms around Cate and Bart's shoulders. He was unbelievably touched by the gift of the locket.

Inside his head, he heard his dad once more.

"Trust the tide, Connor. Make yourself ready. I told you before."

"Yes, Dad," he answered without opening his mouth.

Then he returned to joking with his new friends.

29

DRESSING FOR DINNER

"Why were you so cold to me before?" Grace couldn't help but ask Lorcan the question weighing on her mind.

"What are you talking about?"

Grace hung her head sadly. "You know."

Lorcan was frowning, but his voice was soft now. "I was just trying to get Lieutenant Sidorio away from you. It would have been far better had he not seen you."

"Why?" Grace asked.

"I've told you before, have I not, Grace? This is no ordinary ship and we are no ordinary crew. We may not look so very different from the likes of you, but we have needs you cannot comprehend. Now that you know for yourself what kind of ship this is, I'd have thought you might have been a bit more careful."

"Careful of what?" Grace said, preparing to play her trump card. "The captain told me I was in no danger."

"Really?" Lorcan's eyes pierced deep into her own. "And I suppose he also told you to wander around the deck and introduce yourself to all the crew?"

Grace blushed and dropped her eyes.

"No, no, he didn't."

"I didn't think so."

"He asked me to return here before the Nightfall Bell. But I fell asleep in the galley."

Lorcan stared at her in disbelief.

"You've been into the galley? Grace!"

"Yes," Grace said impatient at his tone. "The captain *did* say I could look around the ship as long as I came back to the cabin before the Nightfall Bell."

"But you chose to disobey the captain."

"No," Grace said firmly, "of course I haven't disobeyed the captain. They gave me some soup in the galley and for some reason it sent me to sleep. I must have slept for a long time because I'd only just woken when the bell started. Even then, I almost made it back here in time, but I ran into Miss Flotsam and she started talking to me and I didn't want to be rude and then, before I knew it . . ."

Lorcan stood up from the chair and pushed it aside angrily. "Before you knew it, you were having a nice cozy chat with Lieutenant Sidorio?"

"I would hardly call it a chat," Grace said, taken aback by Lorcan's aggression.

Lorcan brought his hands up over his eyes, shaking his head despairingly, before dropping his arms again.

"Don't you see? Don't you understand? We're trying to protect you, but you're not helping yourself."

"But what are you protecting me *from*?" Grace asked. "The captain himself told me I was in no danger."

Lorcan sighed, pacing up and down before her as he got his thoughts in order.

"The captain is a fine man, and I would never do anything to flout his authority. He started this ship many years ago and gave me, and others like me, a haven from the darkest reaches of this world. And he looks after us, nurtures us, and gives us a peace we never thought to find again. He sees to our needs with our weekly Feasts. But," he took a deep breath, "there are others on this ship who maybe don't feel that way. They'd sooner not restrict their hunger to one feed a week. They'd sooner decide for themselves how much and how often. They think the time has come to do things differently. And the truth of the matter is, I'm not sure that the captain can make *any* guarantees for your safety anymore."

Lorcan looked sad and almost as shocked as Grace by his own words.

"Until a short time ago, Grace, I'd never have even

thought such things, but you've come to us at a time of great change and nothing is certain now. And here," he prodded his chest, "here, where once I had a heart, I'm starting to think that the sooner we get you off this ship, the better."

Grace looked back at his pained expression. She realized she'd been wrong to ever doubt Lorcan Furey. He truly did seem to have her best interests at heart. But he was starting to scare her now. If he couldn't protect her . . . If even the captain couldn't protect her . . . Then what?

Before she could say anything more, there was a knock at the door. Grace's heart leaped. She and Lorcan both turned toward the door, realizing that he had not locked it behind her this time. And now the globe-shaped handle twisted and the door opened with a creak.

Miss Flotsam swept into the room, trailing the scent of freshly cut roses and clutching several dresses on padded silk coat hangers.

"I said I'd lend you something pretty to wear to the Feast," she said to Grace, "an' I always keep my word."

Lorcan shook his head in a mixture of relief and disbelief.

"Oh shush, you," Miss Flotsam said to him. "If you knew more about the feminine point of view, Midshipman Furey, then you'd know that we ladies like to take pride in our appearance. Isn't that true, Grace?"

Holding each of the dresses up against her in turn, Miss Flotsam scrutinized Grace with the eye of an artist.

"Definitely not the powder blue," she said, letting the discarded dress fall onto the bed and reaching for the next.

Grace didn't much like the look of any of the dresses. She could imagine that they would all look fine on Miss Flotsam but, frankly, Grace was hard pressed to remember the last time she'd worn a dress. And certainly never in her life had she worn any so elaborate as these, with their chiffon and silk and beads and fine pearl buttons.

"I think it's between the pink and the primrose yellow," Miss Flotsam said. "Let's have a gander what you look like in each of them and then we'll decide."

Miss Flotsam began removing the chosen dresses from their hangers. Grace really didn't want to try on either of the gowns. She glanced at Lorcan.

"Grace has no need of such finery," Lorcan said. "She won't be coming to the Feast tonight."

Miss Flotsam turned to Lorcan, confused. "Won't be coming? Why, that's ridiculous! Everyone comes to the Feast."

Lorcan shook his head. "Not Grace," he said.

"That can't be right," Miss Flotsam said, pressing on regardless and offering Grace the primrose gown.

Lorcan reached out and took the dress from her hands. "Grace is *not* coming to the Feast, Darcy. Captain's orders."

He appeared to have said the magic words. Miss Flotsam took the yellow dress back from him and quickly buttoned it up properly. She clutched it to herself, as if bidding a dear friend a reluctant good-bye.

"It's such a pretty dress," Miss Flotsam said sadly.

Grace thought Miss Flotsam might actually cry.

"Why don't you wear the dress yourself, Darcy?" Lorcan said softly.

"Shall I?"

Lorcan nodded. "You go and change into it, but be quick, mind you. I can hear the music beginning."

Grace could hear it, too. It was a strangely soothing piece of percussion. Its main rhythm sounded much like a heartbeat, with a more insistent counterpoint laid over it. Then she remembered the same sounds from her first night on board.

"Yes, I'll go and get changed now," Miss Flotsam said, half talking to herself as she scooped up all the dresses and tottered toward the door.

Before she made it, the door swung open again. Miss Flotsam stopped dead in her tracks. A vast, dark shadow flooded the cabin, blocking out much of the light, as Sidorio stepped across the threshold.

Smiling cruelly, Sidorio cast his malevolent eyes from Miss Flotsam to Grace to Lorcan.

"What's this, Midshipman Furey? I know you're not

much of a man, but are you now debating fashions with the ladies?"

Lorcan said nothing, but moved toward Grace. She felt that he was getting into position to protect her.

"Are you deaf to the music?" Sidorio said. "The Feast is about to begin."

"Indeed," Lorcan said, "and I'm on my way."

"I wasn't talking to you, *Mistress* Furey," Sidorio said. "I was talking to the donor."

His dark eyes were set on Grace. Now she was truly scared. The music had grown louder and the sound of a flute swooped in over the two percussion rhythms.

"Grace isn't a donor," Lorcan said. "There's been a mistake."

"There's been no mistake," Sidorio snarled. "Old Nathaniel's unable to join the Feast tonight. There must be no empty setting at the table. Besides, this scrawny foundling could do with a good meal."

"Grace is *not* a donor," Lorcan said again, squaring up to Sidorio, though the man was at least twice his size.

"And I say she *is*," said Sidorio. "And so says the captain."

Lorcan shook his head. "The captain would never . . ."

"If you don't believe me," Sidorio said, speaking over him, "just go and ask him. In fact, why don't we go together and leave the ladies to their frippery?"

He turned toward Lorcan with a sneer. "Unless, perhaps,

you want to stay behind and dress their hair with pretty ribbons?"

Sidorio chuckled dismissively and walked out of the cabin. Miss Flotsam stood rooted to the spot.

Lorcan turned to Grace, his face torn up in anguish. "I'm so sorry, Grace. I never meant for any of this to happen."

"It's okay," she said, sounding a lot calmer than she felt inside. "It's okay. I know you've done everything you can. If this is how it's meant to be, then so be it. Miss Flotsam, may I have the yellow dress, after all? If I'm coming to the Feast, I may as well look the part."

30

THE FEAST

There was something curiously calming in the music that Grace heard all the more clearly as she stepped out of her cabin in the primrose-yellow dress. It had, of course, been a little long for her — but Miss Flotsam had shown her how to gather the excess and hold it in her hand as she walked along. Stepping down the corridor now, dressed more elegantly than she could ever remember, Grace felt half like a bride and half like a sacrificial lamb. But still, the repetitive drumbeats calmed her.

Miss Flotsam had had to leave her. "Vampires and donors do not enter the Feast together," Lorcan had explained. "The donors arrive first."

And so Grace made her way back down the corridors and stairways of the ship, deeper and deeper into the depths she had explored so eagerly earlier that day. Ahead of her, the other donors emerged from their cabins. They looked, for all intents and purposes, like normal men and women, but there was something languid and listless about them, as if they had already been drained of blood. Which of course they had, on a weekly basis. Evidently, it took its toll — perhaps they would all end up like poor Nathaniel, little more than a frail shell.

The donors all seemed to be older than her. Somehow, that gave her hope — maybe she was too young to be a proper donor. Only, Sidorio didn't seem to think so. On she walked, attempting a nervous smile at the others.

There had been little time following Sidiorio's exit to ask Lorcan everything she had wanted to know. But, as Miss Flotsam had busied herself dressing Grace, Lorcan had told her that he would speak to the captain. He couldn't believe the captain would have changed his mind regarding Grace — it must be some piece of Sidorio's cunning. Lorcan's final words to her had been to remember that even if she was to be a donor, she would not be fatally harmed. That was a matter of opinion, Grace reflected. She understood that she would not be killed — but she would have to give a portion of her blood to another. To Sidorio, perhaps. And, frankly, how much better a fate than death was that?

All these thoughts were pushed aside as she reached the final corridor and followed the other donors into the dining room. It was a vast space, more like an elaborate ballroom, lit by crystal chandeliers, with a long banquet table that stretched far into the distance. It was immaculately laid with damask tablecloths, fine china, cut glass, and sparkling silver cutlery. But it had only been laid along one side.

It was along that side that the donors made their way, coming to a stop before the chairs and standing, waiting while the hypnotic music continued to play. Along the center of the table was a long line of flickering candles. No one spoke.

Then the vampires arrived. Each vampire, Lorcan had explained, was paired with a donor, and now each vampire sought out his or her mate. And, as he or she found the place opposite their donor and made a polite bow, so each pair sat down in their seats.

Grace watched as Miss Flotsam arrived and located the man who was her donor. She curtseyed low and smiled sweetly, before sitting down at the empty place opposite him. Soon after, Grace saw Lorcan enter the room. His face was still troubled and his blue eyes looked anxiously toward her before he found his own donor and bowed formally to the young woman. They too sat down.

So it continued. Each vampire scanned the length of the table and repeated the rather graceful ritual. Grace thought back to her earlier exploration of the ship and her attempt to count the numbers of the crew. There were many more than she had imagined. The dining room must take up almost the entire length of the ship, she thought.

Before long, she was one of only a handful of donors to remain standing. And then there were just two — herself and the man beside her, at the far end of the table.

At last, the final two vampires arrived. Sidorio marched in with characteristic arrogance, some steps ahead of the captain himself. There were only two places left — those opposite Grace and her neighbor. With a growing sense of doom, Grace awaited Sidorio's arrival. When she looked up, there he stood before her. He did not smile and, rather than bowing, merely nodded perfunctorily. There had been a courteous respect in the way the other vampires had treated their donors — an acknowledgment perhaps of the coming sacrifice — but Sidorio showed her none of that. Instead, he pulled out his chair and was about to sit down, when the captain appeared at his side.

"No, Lieutenant, why don't you sit here?"

Grace heard the familiar whisper with relief.

"I'm all right here, Captain. I have chosen my new donor." Sidorio continued to pull out the chair.

"No, Lieutenant, I insist. Change places with me."

And though it was just a whisper, there was no doubting the authority of the captain's words. Sidorio glanced along the length of the table, apparently weighing up his options. The captain waited patiently.

At last, Sidorio stepped aside, barely even nodding to the man at Grace's side, and sat down.

The captain bowed before Grace, then swept up his cloak and sat in the chair in front of her. Grace was unsure if she had been rescued or if she had simply been dealt a different fate. Nevertheless, it gave her some satisfaction to see Sidorio defeated. She smiled at him through gritted teeth.

"Don't bait him, Grace." The captain's words resounded in her head and she turned her focus away again, concentrating on the pulse of the music instead.

~

Dinner was an elaborate affair. No wonder Cook and Jamie had been so stressed at the prospect of it. Each of the donors was served a succession of culinary treats. They began with roasted lobster, which would, Grace thought, have adequately served as a meal in itself. She was still mopping up its delicious juices when her plate was removed and another, laden with steak and a rainbow of vegetables — from tomato through squash to zucchini — replaced it. The meat melted in her mouth, as the lobster had before. Just as earlier, with the soup, Grace felt an extraordinary depth of hunger. And how had Cook been able to prepare so many meals at once, with only Jamie to help her? Truly, it was a mystery.

There was some polite chatter as dinner progressed. But there was no general conversation. The vampires only spoke to their donors, as if, rather than sitting at one long table, they were all at tables for two. Grace could hear Miss Flotsam chattering away, ten to the dozen as usual, giving her donor little chance to respond. Farther along the table, she saw Lorcan smiling and nodding at his young donor. Feeling a pang of envy, she wondered what they might be discussing. She had grown close to Lorcan and it was strange to see him so intimate with another.

Sidorio made no effort at conversation, and even though Grace's neighbor made admirable attempts to draw him out, he just grunted, mumbled indistinguishable words, and drummed his large fingers repeatedly on the tablecloth. His frustration was all too evident to Grace. It was just a matter of time before his rage took flight.

As for the captain, he said little to Grace. He too seemed distracted. Perhaps Sidorio was the cause. It was understandable if Lorcan had been right and Sidorio was on the verge of challenging the captain's authority. But even though the captain did not speak to her, Grace felt somehow safe in his presence. She could recognize the creasing of his mask that indicated a smile. It was sufficient comfort to allow her to enjoy each delicious bite of her meal, without worrying about what might happen next.

All through dinner, the same music played, but somehow it never grew dull or monotonous. After dessert — an intensely flavored fruit jelly — had been cleared away, the music grew louder. For the first time, Grace scanned the length of the room, looking for the musicians. There were none to be seen.

Now the table was clear of crockery on both sides and the music grew louder still. The candles flickered in the center of the table and cast a warm glow from face to face. And now, the vampire and donor at the far end of the table stood, in perfect synchronicity, and exited the dining room together.

Their neighbors followed suit and, like a wave, each pair of vampire and donor raised themselves and made their exit. No one hurried, no one missed a beat. Grace wondered if it was the rhythm of the music that guided them.

At last, it was her turn and, as Sidorio and his donor began their march to the exit, so she and the captain drew themselves up and faced one another again. Turning, they walked down the length of the table, on either side.

Now Grace's heart was beating fast. As much as she tried to bring it into harmony with the steady rhythm of the music, it slipped out of beat like a fish that refuses to be caught.

Finally, as they reached the end of the table, the captain turned and stretched out his arm to Grace. Instinctively, she wound hers through it, as if about to dance with him. They were the last pair to exit the dining room. As they reached the threshold, the captain glanced back over his shoulder and every candle in the room went out at once.

He turned to Grace, staring down at her through his eyeless mask. "Do not be afraid, child," he whispered.

Turning back to follow the others, they continued the ascent to his cabin in silence.

31

THE HUNGER

Back inside his cabin, the captain settled himself in his rocking chair in front of the hearth. He arranged his cape, as he always did, in precise folds. It might, Grace thought, have been a cozy scene. *If* he wasn't the captain of a ship of vampires. *If* he had human eyes and lips and a nose to draw breath in and out of his body — instead of the dark void where those features should have been. *If* in all the other cabins, the rest of the crew were *not* sating their hunger for blood. Yes, but for all these things, it might have been a cozy scene.

And what was *her* fate to be, she wondered, as she watched him stoke the fire, the skin on the back of his head reminding her that he still had some connection to his human form. He had saved her from Sidorio's clutches, yes, but perhaps she had not been rescued so much as swapped. Perhaps he had used his authority as captain to claim her blood for himself. As they had made their way along the corridors of the ship, Grace had seen door after door close as each vampire followed his or her donor into a cabin. The donors entered first, without exception, she noticed. As if they went inside of their own free will. Or, perhaps, so that they were prevented from escaping.

"You're trembling, child. Come and join me by the fire." As before, the words seemed to whisper right inside her head.

As Grace walked tentatively toward him, he turned his masked face toward her.

"Ah, I see that it isn't the cold that makes you tremble so. But why? I've told you that there is nothing to fear."

She thought again of the closing doors. And of the donors' languid resignation to their fate.

"What's going on in the other cabins?"

"Of course, you need to know. Why don't you make yourself comfortable and I'll do my best to answer your questions."

He had this knack of sounding so very reasonable, as if they were talking about a problem with her homework and not about the savage acts that were taking place in the other cabins even as they spoke.

Grace sat down in the rocking chair beside him, but

only at the edge, her feet resting on the floor to keep the chair still.

"As you have seen, child," he said, "each of the members of the crew has a donor. Let me reassure you that the donors are well looked after. They are generously fed and live in comfort."

That, thought Grace, was a matter of opinion. For how could you live in comfort when you knew that you had to offer up your blood to another on a weekly basis?

"It's a good question," the captain said. Grace had forgotten his ease at reading her unspoken thoughts. "But the moment of sharing, as we term it, is not at all painful and actually somewhat brief."

Grace lifted her feet from the floor and swung her legs up, making herself more comfortable. As she relaxed, she started to feel weary and stifled a yawn.

"We feed the donors a very careful diet, extremely high in nutrients. That's why," he noted with a smile, "it can make you a little sleepy."

At his words, Grace jerked upright. The captain continued.

"Such nourishing food can be a shock to the system. But, as you can imagine, it results in very high-quality blood. And that's how we managed to reduce the sharing to once a week. We make a feast of it — a ritual, I suppose — not only to maximize the nutrition content of the blood at the time of sharing, but also to pay tribute to the donors. We are very grateful for their gift — the gift of life. Each week, you see, the crew is reborn."

He paused, and stoked the fire again.

"But what if the other crew members want to take blood in greater quantity, or more often?"

"That is not an option, Grace, not so long as I am their captain. They do not need to feast more often and they do not need any more than a given dose of blood. Taking more would not only endanger the donor, but themselves. It would unbalance them, create . . . what is the term for it? Mood swings. The problem is, the more you take, the more you think you need. But there's the difference, you see — between what you need and what you convince yourself you want."

"But," Grace could not let it go, "what if there were vampires under your command who wanted to take blood in a less controlled way?"

"Then they would have to leave the ship and make their own way in the world. It is not the way we do things here. Vampires are much maligned, Grace. We've been demonized. Why, think of the shanty.

If pirates are danger, and vampires are death . . .

"You know it's true. And of course, I understand why. We've done it to ourselves. We've felt the hunger and based our whole existence on it. But I have found another way. And myself, I no longer even need blood."

This was welcome news to Grace. Her clenched hands slowly began to relax. But how could it be so?

"There are a few of us for whom this is the case. The need for blood is really for *prana,* for energy. I have been taught to feast on that alone."

"So you take *energy* from your donor?"

"I don't *have* a donor, Grace," he said. "And no, nor am I looking for one, so you can relax. The taking of *prana* works a little differently. But it's complicated and I think that's a discussion for another time. Your head must be spinning with all you have seen and heard this night. You look tired and I confess that I feel the same. But let me reassure you that it is a natural fatigue and I have no need to draw energy from you or anyone else. I hope I have given you such reassurances that you can return to your own cabin and rest."

"Yes," Grace said, getting up from the chair. "Yes, you have. Thank you."

"Good." He settled back into his chair and rested his head on his chest.

Behind him, the fire dwindled a little. Grace thought that the veins in his cloak were glowing softly, but perhaps it was just the reflection of the embers.

Quietly, she turned away and walked to the door. As she reached the threshold, his words came into her head again.

"I do so enjoy our talks, Grace."

She smiled. "I do, too. Sleep well."

She pushed open the door and stepped out onto the dark, deserted deck.

A pleasant breeze was blowing and Grace made her way once more to the guardrail. Turning back, she looked up at the ship's winglike sails. The moon was shining low tonight and scattered light onto the sails, making them glow like the captain's cape. She could swear she saw the same veins dimly on the underside of the material. What material *was* this? Was it the same fabric that the captain's cloak was made of?

"The moon is full tonight, is it not?"

She was no longer alone. Without turning around, she recognized the voice. It was Sidorio. Grace's blood ran cold.

"And when the moon is full, I have a high hunger."

As she turned, she saw a horror far worse than she had anticipated. In his thick, heavily veined arms, Sidorio carried a man — the man who had sat opposite him at the Feast. He was sprawled out, and appeared to be sleeping, but a shaft of moonlight revealed that this was a sleep from which he would never wake. Sidorio had drained too much of his blood.

And now, the vampire strode across the red deckboards and, without a moment's hesitation, tossed the corpse over the side of the ship. Grace heard the dull splash as it landed in the water. The sound ricocheted in her head like gunfire. Never had she felt such danger. Never had she felt so completely alone.

Sidorio walked back toward her. As he stepped into the shaft of moonlight, his features were distorted, his eyes once again pits of red fire, like Lorcan's had been and the cook's, too. Clearly, he was still in the dark throes of a terrible hunger. Taking too much from his poor donor had not sated him but, as the captain had foretold, awakened an insatiable appetite.

Grace couldn't run. It was all she could do not to slump to the floor, drained of all energy and resistance.

Sidorio opened his mouth in a horrible smile and the light bounced off his two dagger-sharp gold teeth.

"Let's go to your cabin," he said.

32

MA KETTLE'S TAVERN

Bart and Cate had not lied. Ma Kettle's Tavern was unlike any place Connor had ever been before. As he jumped down onto the dockside, Bart slapped him on the back.

"Welcome to the dark side," he whispered in Connor's ear. "What d'ya think of the place?"

It truly was incredible — a cross between an old pub and a pier. It was set on wooden stilts some ten feet or more above the water and looked completely unstable, as if at any moment the whole structure might collapse in on itself and sink into the sea. At the back of the structure rose a vast waterwheel, sloshing noisily as it revolved, like a sea monster guzzling the ocean water then spewing it out again.

As Connor followed Bart and Cate into the tavern, he glanced down between his feet. There were patches of apparently solid decking, on which stood long tables and benches. But, between these, there were vast gaps in the flooring, which gave way to the waters below. It was unclear whether the wood had rotted away over time, or if there just hadn't been enough to complete the floor in the first place.

It would, thought Connor, be easy to fall through these, and indeed, as he walked carefully along, he looked down to see more than one worse-for-wear pirate flailing about in the water. Ropes hung down from the wooden beams at regular intervals, presumably to help the fallen pirates climb back up again — if they were able. Otherwise, it was a premature end to their night out.

The fearless serving girls ran along the narrow rafters, as nimble and sure of foot as gymnasts, carrying foaming mugs of beer to the waiting pirate crews. But, as agile as they were, the girls were not to be messed with. Bart nudged Connor as Toothless Jack whispered something in one of the server's ears. She leaned back, smiled at him, and then shoved him firmly down into the water. Stepping away from the splash-back, the girl continued on her way, giving Bart and Connor a wink.

"That should sober him up," she said.

"Actually, he hasn't *started* drinking yet," Bart said.

The girl shook her head and laughed. "I'll see you guys later. If you need anything, anything at all, just ask for Sugar Pie."

She continued on her way and the lads turned to watch her, spellbound.

"I think I'm in love," Connor said, his eyes wide as saucers.

"Ooh dear," Bart said, "I think we've finally found something to fall out about."

"Stop dawdling, boys," cried Molucco Wrathe, putting his arms around their shoulders and propelling them forward. "Ma Kettle's reserved us a table or three in her VIP section. Let's round up the crew and get the party started . . . before Mistress Li tells us it's against regulations!"

As far as Connor could see, the party was already in full swing. Above the noise of the waterwheel was that of the band, playing very loud music — a strange blend of jazz, rock, and sea shanty. Connor had never heard anything like it before, but it was noisy and it was fun, just like everything else around here.

Just as Captain Wrathe had said, a section of long tables had been roped off up ahead. In the center of the tables, Connor noticed a heavy wooden marker with a painting of *The Diablo* on it. *Reserved for Captain Wrathe and his crew,* read the script underneath the picture.

"All the major players have these," Bart told Connor. "Like I told ya, this is the hot spot for pirate crews from miles around. There's really no place like it."

They sat down at a table and, almost immediately, two

mugs of foaming beer were placed in front of them. Bart lifted his tankard in the air.

"Bottoms up!"

"Wait a minute!" It was Cutlass Cate. "Should Connor be drinking beer?"

"Of course he shouldn't," said Captain Wrathe, joining them. "He's far too young. Get this boy a hot rum punch!"

Cate shook her head in disbelief, then smiled.

"Has everyone got a drink?" Captain Wrathe called.

"Aye, Cap'n," came the roar from down the long table — now packed with members of his thirsty crew.

"Excellent!" cried Captain Wrathe, jumping up onto the table.

"A toast then, if you please, my fellows. To a most satisfactory day's pirating and to the finest crew of pirates that ever sailed the seas!"

"*What* did you say, Wrathe?"

Connor turned just in time to see one of the other pirate captains leap onto a neighboring table, his heavy boots booming like thunder as he landed.

The band decided this was too good to miss and stopped their music to watch.

Looking around, Connor saw that another three ferocious-looking pirates had also leaped onto the tables around them. Six more followed suit.

Unabashed, Captain Wrathe beamed. "Why, good evening, my fellow captains. I see Ma has a full house to-night! And how, pray, are we all faring on this balmy evening?"

"We were faring handsomely until you arrived," one of the others shouted. The man's crew roared with laughter and drummed their feet on the deck in approval. "And we'd be faring better yet if you stopped steering your poxy ship into our sea lanes!"

"That's right!" cried another of the captains. "The rest of us play by the rules, but you just zigzag around the ocean like a drunken whale."

There was more laughter, but it had a nasty edge.

"Fellows," Captain Wrathe said, attempting to maintain a jocular tone, "perhaps I have been a little naughty of late, but is this the place —"

"Naughty?" snarled the first pirate. "You're not going to get out of this that easily."

"That's right," said the second. "We want back what's rightfully ours."

"What's rightfully yours?"

"Booty, Wrathe. We know for a fact you went fishing in our sea lane today. And everything you took now belongs to us."

At this, the man's own crew whooped in approval and began bashing their tankards on the table.

"And so shall ye reap," muttered Cheng Li.

Connor saw Cate give her an angry look. With the increasing clamor, he was starting to fear not just for Captain Wrathe's safety but for the fragile structure of the tavern.

Captain Wrathe seemed a little shaken but he soon recovered his composure. "I'm sorry to have offended, my fine fellows, and come morning, let us meet and make amends. Yes? It's hard to teach a salty old dog new tricks, but I shall try to mend my wanton ways. But tonight, let's have no trouble, eh?"

He looked from one of the other captains to the next. They were stony faced, but he called back, "Won't you join me in a toast? Come on, let no man take against me tonight — for I'm in a sentimental mood. Come on, raise your glasses!"

Connor looked around the tavern. Every single table had stopped its noise and horseplay. Every pirate's attention was focused on Captain Wrathe. Connor remembered Bart telling him that Molucco Wrathe had something of a reputation and clearly he had not been wrong.

"Here's to the life of a pirate," Captain Wrathe cried, turning as he spoke to include all the crews. "A short life but a merry one!"

He drained his tankard of beer in a single go. Quickly, Sugar Pie took away his empty tankard and replaced it with a full one.

There was a moment's silence in the tavern and then the other captains and crews lifted their tankards and shouted together, "A short life but a merry one!"

There was much drumming of feet and slamming down of tankards as every man and woman in the tavern took part in the toast. The whole building trembled.

Captain Wrathe held his hand aloft and silenced the uproar.

"Where's Ma Kettle?" he shouted. "I want to buy every last rascal in this tavern another drink. You may think the captain of *The Diablo* is a fool, but let no man say he is an ungenerous fool!"

There was another noisy cheer and, without missing a beat, the serving girls clambered along the rafters, their hands improbably balancing clusters of overflowing tankards. Once again, Connor watched in awe, never having seen anything like this spectacle.

"Well, look who's rolled in with the tide," came a distinctive, smoky voice, "and made enough of a racket to rouse me from my beauty sleep."

Bart nudged Connor, who slopped his drink over the table and onto his boots. "You don't want to miss this, mate!"

Connor turned, just in time to see a striking woman in a vast black ballgown swaggering toward their table. As she came nearer, Connor saw that her outfit was made entirely of skull-and-crossbone flags, sewn together. Ma Kettle was older than her "girls" but she was a fine-looking woman with jewel-like eyes and a shock of blood-red hair, in which she wore a tiara in the shape of a cutlass.

"Give a girl a leg up," she said, as she reached their table.

With no further urging, six pirates leaped up, stretched out their hands, and lifted Ma Kettle onto the table.

"Why, thank you, gentlemen," she said, gracefully curtsying to them before continuing along the table to greet Captain Wrathe.

"It's been a while, Lucky," she said, warmly embracing him. Captain Wrathe's sapphire-studded fingers clutched her tenderly to him.

As Ma Kettle hugged Captain Wrathe, Connor saw that on the back of her dress was a rendering of the skull and crossbones in sparkling rhinestones. On a lesser character it might have looked tacky, but Ma Kettle was pure rock and roll.

"Kitty," Captain Wrathe said, stepping back and beaming at her, their fingers still entwined. "My sweet Kitty, as beauteous now as when first we met. When was that now? Do you recall?"

"Let's not put a date on it, eh?" said Ma Kettle, smiling prettily. "But of course I remember the day I first clapped eyes on my Lucky. You were the most handsome pirate I had ever seen. And frankly, my darling, the years have only made you more delicious, you old rogue."

Connor was surprised to see Captain Wrathe blush tomato-red.

"Kitty, my dear, I have a new crew member. A very special lad whom I should like to introduce to you."

He pointed down toward the bench where Connor sat between Bart and Cate.

"Ooh, hello, Bartholomew," said Ma Kettle, waving. "Now *there's* a beautiful man. If I was ten years younger . . . all right, maybe twenty or thirty or so."

Bart blew Ma Kettle a kiss and she mimed a catch.

"All right, Kitty, but look past that handsome devil Bartholomew to his young neighbor. Mister Tempest, come up and be presented to pirate royalty."

Connor stood up, finding himself a little wobbly on his feet. Carefully, he climbed up onto the table and approached Ma Kettle. Not knowing exactly what to do, and already a little worse for wear, he decided to bow.

"Well, aren't you a treasure?" Ma Kettle said. "A fine young pirate, I can tell. And, believe me, I've seen a few. You stick with Lucky, young man, and you won't go far wrong."

She winked at Connor, then called over her shoulder. "Sugar Pie, my angel, make sure the girls are extra nice to young Mister Tempest tonight. And if any other pirate gives the boy so much as an ounce of trouble, give him a punch and tell him he's barred until spring!"

"Aye, aye, Ma," called Sugar Pie, giving her boss a cheeky salute.

"Thank you," Connor mumbled, blushing. He climbed down, rather embarrassed by the attention.

Ma Kettle led Captain Wrathe off for a private chat and a dance. "Come on," she cried at the band. "Start playing! I don't pay you to stand and gawp!"

"You don't pay us at all," cried the bass player.

"Oh, shut up, Johnny, and play!"

Connor laughed. He felt a tap on his shoulder. He turned around to see Cheng Li standing behind him.

"Let's walk and talk," she said.

Connor stood up, still feeling a bit wobbly.

"You should leave your beer here, buddy," said Bart, chuckling.

Cheng Li led Connor away from the main bar, off along a boardwalk lined with jacaranda trees, strung with twinkling lights. It was deserted but for them, and quieter as they moved away from the bar.

"It's been one full week since I rescued you, boy," Cheng Li said. "And a lot has happened in that week."

"Yes," Connor agreed.

"You have impressed me greatly, boy. Today, most of all."

He swelled at her praise.

"You showed great bravery today, but also, you showed mercy."

He wasn't entirely sure if that was a compliment coming from her.

"I said some things to you before the raid. Things that I should perhaps not have burdened you with. We must each fight our own battles. I am, after all, deputy captain." She rubbed her jeweled armband as if to add more luster to the gem.

"We're part of a team," Connor said. "I was flattered you confided in me. And I would never discuss what you said with anyone."

Cheng Li stopped for a moment in her tracks. She looked directly at him.

"That would be deeply appreciated, boy."

"No problem," Connor said. For the first time, he felt he was speaking to her on something like a level footing.

"The thing that impresses me most about you, Connor, is the way you haven't let your grief for your sister cloud your actions."

He smiled. "Ah, but you see, I know she's all right. She's coming back soon."

"What do you mean? I do not understand." Her dark eyes frowned in confusion.

Connor smiled as he spoke. "My dad told me. I don't have to wait much longer. Grace is alive and we'll be reunited soon."

"But your father is — forgive me — dead." Still her face was masked with incomprehension.

"Yes, but sometimes I hear his voice."

"You hear the voice of a dead man?"

"Yes. You probably think it's crazy."

"No." She shook her head. "No, my mind is quite open to such things. And what exactly has he told you?"

"Not much," Connor acknowledged. "To make myself ready and to trust the tide."

"Trust the tide. That's interesting."

"I thought I might be imagining it, but I really don't think so. It's so clearly his voice. And I feel it in my heart. Grace is okay. I know she is." As he mentioned her name, he thought he felt the locket under his shirt vibrate slightly.

"So, Connor Tempest, your bravery is not your lone talent. Once more, I am impressed. I wonder — does your sister share some of these prodigious talents?"

"Oh, yes," Connor said. "She's much smarter than me. She reads books and she has this knack for reading people, too. And she's strong — not so much physically, but mentally. Grace never gives up."

Cheng Li nodded. They had reached the end of the boardwalk and stood at the edge of the water. "She sounds like an extraordinary young woman. I greatly look forward to meeting her."

Cheng Li turned toward Connor. "I told you before, Connor. The world of piracy is changing. There are fantastic opportunities for people like you and Grace. Opportunities that would blow your mind to even think about."

Connor was immediately intrigued and ready to hear more.

"We will talk again. For now, we must go back and join the others," Cheng Li said, her eyes twinkling. "I shall buy you a cup of hot rice wine and we will toast to our brilliant future."

They started the walk back.

"One more thing," Cheng Li said.

"Yes."

"I think we'll keep this conversation to ourselves, Connor. I know that you have many friends on *The Diablo,* and that's good — of course it is. But there are some things people like you and I cannot share with others. It is the burden of our greatness. I see a brilliant future for you. You will easily surpass those you see as comrades now — even people you see as superiors. It won't be an easy journey — do not expect it to be. But the easy journeys are not worth the leather on the soles of our shoes, boy. It's the journeys that test us to our very core — the journeys that strip the clothes from our back, mess with our minds, and shake our spirits — these are the journeys worth taking in life. They show us who we are."

Her words were typically brutal, but as they continued on their way in companionable silence, Connor thought he already knew something of what she meant.

33

THE END OF MY STORY

Grace did not struggle. What was the point? Sidorio was too strong. He shut her cabin door behind them and turned the key in the lock, slipping it into his pocket for safekeeping.

He filled the room, not just physically, but with an aura of threat and violence. Suddenly, it was no longer her sanctuary but a place of danger. This, she realized, might be where her story came to a sudden and brutal end.

She was all too conscious of the silence outside. There had been no sign of the others when she left the captain's cabin. The night had ended early, on account of the shar-ing. The captain was asleep. Lorcan was feeding. Even if she screamed now, no one would hear her. No one could get to her quickly enough. The only person who could hope to save her now was herself. But how?

"What is it that you want from me?" she asked, deciding to begin with the worst.

Sidorio smirked at her. "I want your blood, of course," he said.

His directness could, she supposed, be looked upon as refreshing. He was perhaps the only person she'd encountered on the ship who was not given to speaking in riddles.

"But why mine?"

He shrugged. "Because it's there. And I'm hungry."

She could see it in his face. It was as if it was made of candle wax, melting and shifting. She had seen this look before — first on Lorcan and then just a moment ago, outside. This must be the face they all had behind the closed doors, as the hunger rose within them, breaking through them like a wave.

"But you could get much better blood than mine," Grace said, having a sudden brainwave. "I'm new to the ship. I've only eaten one proper meal since I arrived. My blood must be the least nutritious of anybody's! You could do much better."

Her words seemed to have struck home with him. He looked at her curiously for a moment. Then he shook his head.

"Blood is blood."

"That's not what the captain told me," she said.

The mere mention of the captain made Sidorio grimace. Perhaps it had been unwise to mention him but she was running out of ideas.

"The captain likes to make up little rules," Sidorio said. "He likes his weekly *dinner parties*. Likes us to suppress our natural appetite, to pretend we're civilized. But you know what? We're *not* civilized. We're vampires, demons . . . call us what you will. And vampires need blood. Pure and simple."

"Ah, but do you *really* need it?" Grace said. "It looks to me like you have already feasted tonight. Maybe you don't need any more." She remembered the captain's words. "I know you are hungering for it, but you don't really *need* it. You just want it."

"Need. Want. What's the difference?" He yawned. "You're boring me."

Grace had retreated as far away from Sidorio as she could. Her back was pinned against the desk. As she leaned back still farther, the stack of notebooks and pencils tumbled onto the floor. As they fell, she had a sudden idea.

"Tell me your story," she said.

"What?" He looked at her strangely.

"Tell me how you crossed. Who you were before. What your life was like."

He stared at her blankly. Was his mortal life so long ago that he had forgotten? The others had seemed eager to rekindle their life story. But he was not like the others.

He seemed to have lost all traces of his humanity. Or had he?

"I was a pirate," he said, eyes suddenly sparking. "In a place called Cilicia in the first century BC." He smiled. "Now that was the place and time to be a pirate. We controlled the whole of the Mediterranean and brought the Roman Empire to its knees."

As he warmed to his story, Grace took the risk of indicating the chair. She was a little surprised to find he followed her lead and sat down in it.

"We had a very healthy slave trade going on," Sidorio continued. "Slaves — that was my specialty. We let the wealthy ones buy their freedom and then we took the others to market. Made a fortune."

He nodded, as if one memory was opening up another. Then, just as suddenly, he snapped out of his reverie.

"Why do you want to know this?"

"I'm collecting crossing stories," Grace said, thinking on her feet. "I thought I might write them down. Miss Flotsam told me hers earlier, and Lorcan."

"Mine's better," Sidorio said. "Mine's the best."

Grace couldn't help but smile. She had tapped into a rich vein of arrogance.

"Tell me," she said, "tell it all to me." She picked up a notebook and pencil. At first, her hand quivered, but somehow she overcame that and began taking notes.

"You've heard of Julius Caesar?"

She nodded.

"Arrogant Roman scum," Sidorio snarled. "We kidnapped him, me and my buddies."

Grace's eyes widened. This really *was* interesting. She hadn't paid much attention in school, but she was sure she'd have remembered this.

"Arrogant piece of dirt, he was. Fancied himself a scholar, was off to study rhetoric, whatever that is, on Rhodes. We took his ship off Pharmacusa Island. Held him hostage. Even then, he was full of himself, telling us he was the big man. Even when we ransomed him, said he'd pay us more than double out of his own pocket to set him free."

Sidorio sighed. "Some of the men were weak, won over by his boasts. They forgot he was our prisoner. I never did. He hated me." Sidorio smiled. "Called me every name under the sun. Threatened me with all sorts. He loved to talk big."

Sidorio went quiet again. Grace turned the page and looked up at him. He had to keep talking. That was the trick. As long as he kept talking, she could buy herself more time. She'd keep him talking until daybreak if she had to, and then expose him to the sunlight.

"What happened then?" she asked.

"His ransom was paid," Sidorio said. "Turns out he was the big man after all. Should have known that really. We set him ashore at Miletus, did a deal with the governor to postpone our trial."

He stopped again.

"And then?"

"And then" — Sidorio fixed her with his dark eyes — "and then Caesar took the law into his own hands. He came back for us and took his revenge. He killed me."

"You were killed by Caesar?"

Sidorio nodded, smiling. "I told you my story was the best."

He glanced over at the notebook, apparently pleased to see how her writing had covered the pages. He took the book from her hands and gazed at it. She wasn't sure if he was actually reading it. Then he threw it onto the floor.

"I'm bored again," he said. "And I'm hungry. Come over here."

She shook her head.

If he was going to take her blood, let him come to her. She felt numb. Was this to be it then? Because she knew that when Sidorio drank, that would be the end of her. He was like an animal who'd been caged for too long, suddenly free, with time to make up. If he took her blood now, he would inflict on her all the savagery he had been denied for so long, she was sure.

He stood and came toward her. In spite of herself, she found herself cowering. *No, please no, not here, not like this.*

Sidorio reached out and his hand pushed the hair back

from her neck. His touch was gentle but her terror was like a bolt of lightning slicing through her. All the fears she had somehow pushed down during her time on the ship were suddenly unleashed. Adrenaline ripped through her body like fireworks. And then, just as suddenly, everything was calm again and she felt as if she was utterly numb, floating.

At that moment, a strange noise entered the room. A humming. It filled the room, growing louder until Sidorio too paused to listen to it. Where was it coming from? Outside or inside? It was not quite clear. Whichever, it was growing louder and louder. And now, as the humming grew loud enough to burst their eardrums, the wall behind Sidorio seemed to buckle and shake.

A swarm of insects broke through the wall. As they filled the room, the walls grew still again but the noise was unbearable. Grace put her hands to her ears and Sidorio did the same. Grace watched with amazement as the black horde of tiny creatures encircled Sidorio, who raised his hands tightly around his head. The insects burrowed into his eyes and ears, wrapping him in a dark cloak. And then, right before Grace's eyes, she realized that Sidorio was no longer encircled by the creatures but by a dark cloak of a leathery material, with glowing veins that pulsated as if they were breathing.

"Sidorio," said the captain, releasing him from his clutches. "You will leave the ship now."

Sidorio offered neither fight nor protest. He seemed, despite his hatred for the captain, to finally accept that his rival's powers were superior to his own. Just as, in the end, he had known that Caesar was a mightier, cleverer man.

⌒

Sidorio stood at the guardrail opposite Grace and the captain. The deck was deserted but for them. The captain's gloved hand rested comfortingly on Grace's shoulder.

Sidorio shook his head, smiling. "Don't you have a little leaving ceremony for me, Captain?"

"This gives me no satisfaction," the captain said, "but you have left me no alternative. Your ways are not the ways of this ship."

"No," Siodorio said. "No, they're not."

"As of this moment," the captain said, "you are no longer a Vampirate. I can no longer have you aboard this ship." He looked out into the distance. "Though I shudder to think what havoc you will wreak out there."

"Well, prepare to be dazzled!" Sidorio said, climbing up onto the guardrail.

He glanced from the captain to Grace.

"This isn't the last of me," he said. "This isn't the end of my story."

With that, he turned and dived off the ship, deep into the ocean. Grace looked down as the dark waters received him.

"Come, Grace," the captain said, drawing her away, "let's go back inside."

———

Before she'd had the chance to take in these incredible events, Grace heard the sound of feet running along the deck and there, suddenly, was Lorcan. He looked panic-stricken and out of breath.

"Grace, thank goodness. I went past your cabin and I saw the door was open. I saw blood on deck. And Sidorio is nowhere to be found . . . I thought . . . I couldn't help but think . . ."

"As you can see, Midshipman Furey, Grace is safe and well. It appears that I owe you an apology, however. I thought you were being overprotective of Grace, but it appears I do not know my own crew as well as I thought. Sidorio ended the life of his donor tonight."

"But," said Lorcan, his mind racing to catch up, "what happened? Where is his donor? Where is Sidorio now? Did he hurt you, Grace?"

"The book is closed, Midshipman Furey," said the captain. As ever, though his words were only whispers, his authority was without question. He stood up.

Grace shuddered, thinking again of Sidorio throwing the donor's blood-sapped corpse over the side of the ship. Now the captain, too, was drawing a veil over it. Was life really so disposable?

"I do not want Grace put in any more danger during her stay on the ship. I'm making you her official protector. Do not let her out of your sight. Do everything you can to see that she comes to no harm. Do you understand?"

Lorcan nodded soberly. "You have my word, Captain. With the last of my breath, I shall fight to protect her."

34

THE STRANGER

It was late in the night when the swimmer heaved himself up onto the dockside. His limbs were a little tired but mostly he felt renewed energy and a definite satisfaction at his exertion. He was pumped in a way he could not remember. His mind was racing as much as the energy bubbling through every cell in his body.

He drew himself up to his full height and glanced back at the dark ocean, through which he had journeyed. He'd seen altogether too much of that ocean. It felt good to be back on dry land. He turned away and looked up along the boardwalk.

There were lights flickering ahead and the clamor of voices. Then came a single voice, singing. He began walking toward it, trying to catch the words that drifted through the night air.

I'll tell you a tale of Vampirates,
A tale as old as true.
Yea, I'll sing you a song of an ancient ship,
And its mighty fearsome crew.
Yea, I'll sing you a song of an ancient ship
That sails the oceans blue . . .
That haunts the oceans blue.

It was a boy's voice, the swimmer registered. A voice that was just starting to break. Up ahead lay the inn. His sense of direction had been as flawless as ever. This was the place. This was where all the pirates gathered. And, though it was late in the night, here they were, clustered around a young boy with a breaking voice who sang a song to an old melody.

The Vampirate ship has tattered sails
That flap like wings in flight.
They say that the captain, he wears a veil
So as to curtail your fright

At his death-pale skin
And his lifeless eyes
And his teeth as sharp as night.
Oh, they say that the captain, he wears a veil
And his eyes never see the light.

You'd better be good, child – good as gold,
As good as good can be.
Else I'll turn you in to the Vampirates
And wave you out to sea.

There was something about the boy, something familiar. He couldn't work out exactly what it was. His head
was throbbing. The exertion of the long swim was starting to catch up with him. So too was his hunger. A hunger
such as he had not felt for a long, long time.

Yes, you'd better be good, child – good as gold,
Because – look! Can you see?
There's a dark ship in the harbor tonight
And there's room in the hold for thee!
(Plenty of room for thee!)

The boy had seen him now and though he continued the song, he let a note or two slide, distracted by the swimmer's heavy footprints. And who wouldn't have been distracted by a stranger such as this? A stranger whose very height and muscled build was enough to block out even the moonlight.

Well, if pirates are bad,

And vampires are worse,

Then I pray that as long as I be,

That though I sing of Vampirates,

I never one shall see.

Yea, if pirates are danger,

And vampires are death,

I'll extend my prayer for thee —

That thine eyes never see a Vampirate . . .

. . . and they never lay a hand on thee.

His song finished, the boy stood there, staring at the swimmer, who had stopped just a few paces short of the table. Now others turned around to see what had caught the boy's attention. Suddenly, they were all looking at him.

He opened his mouth. *"I'll tell you a tale of Vampirates,"* he said.

And then panic combined with exhaustion and hunger and his vision blurred. And everything went dark.

＊＊＊

Connor looked down at the stranger, as Bart poured another drop of rum into his mouth. The man was soaked through. Where had he come from at this time of night? His clothes were strange, out of place and time. And he had looked so strangely at Connor as he'd sung the Vampirate shanty. Perhaps it had distressed him and that was why he had fainted.

With a splutter, the man came back to life, turning to spit out the rum.

"Here, buddy, have some more, it'll do ya good," Bart said.

The stranger shook his head and turned his face away. "No more."

"Would you rather have some water?" asked Cate, close by.

"Nothing," the stranger said slowly.

And, curiously, now that he had returned to consciousness, he did seem to have fully recovered. He even shunned their offers of help to lift him, easing himself up and onto the bench nearby.

"What's your name, stranger?" Captain Wrathe asked. "Where have you come from?"

The stranger said nothing, but turned back to look at the ocean.

"Have you come from another ship?" Bart asked.

"Give him time to answer," Captain Wrathe said. "He seems to be in shock."

"It was the shanty," Connor said. "He heard me singing about the Vampirates."

At the mention of the word, the stranger spun his head toward Connor.

"Vam-pi-rates," he said very slowly.

Connor could not breathe, such was his anticipation.

"I'll tell you a tale of Vampirates," the man said, his voice low and cracked.

Connor could not hold back any longer. "I'm looking for a ship. The Vampirate ship. Have you come from it?"

Connor felt the locket vibrating against his pounding heart. This *had* to be the breakthrough. This *had* to be his way back to Grace.

But the man looked at him with wide, empty eyes.

Connor could not let go. "I think my sister is on that ship. She's my age. We're twins. Her name is Grace."

The stranger's expression had altered even before Connor had finished speaking. His mouth had broken into a smile at the mention of Grace. A smile of recognition, perhaps. And now he was looking into Connor's eyes and nodding. "You're twins. Grace."

He *did* know something. Connor was so full of questions, he did not know what to ask next. Before he had a chance to speak, he heard Cheng Li's voice.

"Tell us about the Vampirates," she said. "How can we fight them? Will they try to take our blood?"

The stranger looked at her in wonder, frowning, as if in pain. Then he nodded.

"Did they take *your* blood?" she asked, with a rare softness. "Is that it? Were you a prisoner of the Vampirates? Did they take your blood before you escaped? Is that why you're so weak?"

"Blood," was all he said before his eyes closed again.

"No," Connor cried. "Please, sir, don't let go now. We need you to tell us where that ship is. We need to know if my sister is there."

"Grace," said the stranger, then, "danger."

"Come on," Captain Wrathe said. "There's no time to lose. Round up the crew and prepare the ship. We'll take him with us."

Captain Wrathe looked down at the poor stranger, whose eyes flickered for a moment, then closed.

"They must be terrible demons to weaken such a strong man as this," Captain Wrathe said sadly. "If only we knew the chink in their armor. If only we had a clue."

The stranger's eyes flickered again and he clutched Connor's arm with his hand.

"He has something to tell us," Bart said. "Maybe if I try some more rum?"

The stranger shook his head and squeezed Connor's arm again. Though he was weak, his grip was strong and Connor flinched at the pain.

"What is it?" Connor asked. "What is it that you want so badly to tell us?"

"Attack when night becomes day . . ." He seemed to struggle to get the words out. "At their weakest in the light."

The effort of the words was too much for him and his eyes closed and once more he slumped back against the table.

Connor thought he would explode. At last, at last he had his clue to finding Grace! But what if it was too late? What if they had feasted on her and weakened her like this? What if they had left only a fragile shell?

"Connor," Captain Wrathe said, spotting his concern. "You keep steady, do you hear me? Believe that she's all right. And trust me, my young friend, we will take our revenge for whatever they have done to her. This man has given us a great gift. He'll take us to their ship and we'll do the rest. We're going to find your sister, my boy, and we're going to destroy these demons."

Lying there on the bench, his eyes shut tight, Sidorio wanted to do nothing so much as laugh. These poor fools had swallowed his performance hook, line, and sinker. He had forgotten how much fun it could be playing with mortals' minds. And he couldn't wait to see the Vampirate captain's reaction when a ship of vengeful pirates arrived at daylight. Could revenge really be so easy as this? For the first time in a long, long time, he awaited dawn with delicious anticipation.

35

IT BEGINS

Lorcan and Grace stood on the deck of the ship. Grace had been reluctant to return directly to her cabin after what had happened there with Sidorio.

"We could go back to *my* cabin, if you prefer," Lorcan said, "but we must go back inside soon."

"No, no, I'll be okay. I have to go back there sometime. Just a few minutes more, though," she said. "It's so beautiful tonight with all the stars."

"All right, but just a few minutes more. It's getting late and the sky is beginning to lighten. We must be inside before Darcy sounds the Dawning Bell!"

Grace nodded. She remembered how he had cowered from the light in her cabin before. She would not put him through that pain again.

The Diablo coursed through the open waters, in pursuit of the Vampirate ship. The stranger had recovered sufficiently to give the captain directions, though he had struggled to remember his own name. At last, he had turned to Captain Wrathe with a flicker of a smile and said, "Caesar." Now "Caesar" was at the captain's side, while Connor, Bart, Cate, and Cheng Li stood close by.

The deck was packed tight with members of the crew. News had spread fast that Connor's twin sister was alive but in grave danger, and every pirate was preparing for the fight of their lives. Connor was touched by their unwavering support.

"You're one of us now, Connor," Captain Wrathe told him, "and every pirate looks out for his brother."

Cutlass Cate and Cheng Li gave the crew a joint briefing, telling them to beware of an enemy they knew next to nothing about. Cate had pressed Caesar for what information he had, but he just kept repeating, "Attack as night becomes day and victory will be yours."

At last, they saw the shadow of a ship up ahead. That must be it. The captain turned to Caesar expectantly. He nodded. Connor's heart was beating fast. Bart placed a hand on his friend's shoulder. "Not long now, buddy," he said.

The deck of the ship seemed to be quiet. Captain Wrathe slowed the speed of *The Diablo* to reduce the noise. He wanted to make the most of the element of surprise. The cannons were loaded and the Three Wishes were half-suspended in readiness. Soon merry hell would break loose — but until the last possible moment, he wanted silence.

Finally, the captain turned to Cate. "Please make the final preparations for attack."

"Not yet," interrupted Caesar. "Too dark."

"We can't take the chance of waiting any longer," said Captain Wrathe. "You've been wonderfully helpful, Caesar, but we'll take our chances now."

"Besides," Cheng Li said, "look, the light is coming from the east."

Caesar trembled, his eyes flickering again as they had at the tavern.

"Are you all right?" Cheng Li asked.

"I'm a little cold," he said, his eyes almost shut. "Perhaps if my work is done, I might go inside for a while and rest."

Captain Wrathe nodded.

"I'll help you to a cabin," Cheng Li said, reaching out her arm and leading the poor, broken invalid across the deck.

Captain Wrathe turned to Cate again. "Make the preparations, Cate. Now."

"No."

Connor stepped forward.

The others turned to him questioningly.

"Look, the deck is almost deserted. I can see only two figures and I think one of them is Grace. Let's do things differently. Let me go in there alone."

Cate shook her head. "You can't do that, Connor. I'm sorry, but you just don't have enough experience of combat. And besides, we don't want to lose you."

"I'm sure that's Grace," Connor said. "If we charge in, it will scare whoever's with her and who knows what he'll do. Maybe if I just go in myself, I can quietly take him out without alerting the rest of the crew."

"It's too dangerous," Cate said.

But Captain Wrathe shook his head. "It's Connor's call. It's his sister on that ship and we must do things his way."

Connor smiled at the captain. "Thank you," he said, immensely grateful.

"How about I come along as backup, buddy?"

"No, Bart. Thanks for the offer, but this is something I must do alone."

"At least take this," Cate said, passing Connor her precious rapier.

"I can't," Connor said.

"Don't make me pull rank on you," Cate said, placing the handle in Connor's gloved hands.

"Thank you, thank you all."

Cate went to tell the waiting pirates that there had been a change of plan.

Connor stood at the front of the ship, between Captain Wrathe and Bart.

"The moment I saw you, Mister Tempest, I knew you were a hero in the making," said the captain. "But you know what? You already are one."

Connor heard the words but could not respond to them. The ship was almost alongside its neighbor now and he had to stay utterly focused on the deck ahead. Everything he had been through had brought him to this moment. He had seen Grace, at least he was pretty sure he had seen her. But now the deck was utterly empty.

Above him, the pirates carefully drew down one of the wishes. They had oiled it after the last attack and it was much quieter now. Still, every scrape of metal made Connor's skin crawl. Nothing must alert the Vampirates that he was coming. Nothing must lessen his chance of success.

As soon as the wish was horizontal, he turned toward Captain Wrathe, Bart, and Cate, who had rejoined them. There was no time for dramatic good-byes. Besides, he'd be back in a short time. Wouldn't he?

"Get a bloody move on," said Bart. "We want to meet your sister while she's still a young woman!"

With a smile, Connor jumped onto the wish and ran across it to the other deck.

"What was that?" Lorcan asked Grace.

"What was what?"

"That noise."

"I didn't hear anything."

Lorcan frowned. "Someone's out on deck. I heard foot-steps."

"It'll be Miss Flotsam," Grace said. "She'll be off to ring the Dawning Bell."

"No, Darcy's more fleet-footed than that. Those are a man's boots. There's a man out there."

Grace's eyes widened. "Not Sidorio?"

"I pray not," Lorcan said, "but I'd better check."

"You can't go out now," Grace said. "It'll be light in a few minutes. I don't know where Miss Flotsam can have got to."

"Something isn't right," Lorcan said. "I'm going out. You close the door and stay here."

He pushed open the door of Grace's cabin and darted out onto the deck. She followed him.

Connor continued along the deck, as quietly as he could. It was still empty as far as he could see, though he could hear muffled noises across the other side. He heard a girl's voice.

"Grace," he said, unable to stop the word coming out.

"Connor?"

She had called his name. As clear as day. She was alive! He was in time. He ran around the side of the ship.

There she was.

"Connor," she said, raising her hands to her head in disbelief.

It was then that Connor saw the man at her side. No, not a man — a Vampirate. He gripped his sword in readiness and ran toward them.

—⁓—

Lorcan was troubled to find Grace had followed him on the deck, and even more so to see a stranger running toward them, sword in hand.

"It's Connor," Grace called breathlessly. "It's my brother. He's found me at last!"

It took a moment for Lorcan to compute her words, and then, as the lad came closer, he saw that it all made sense. They were twins. They were not identical, but there was a clear resemblance. Lorcan stepped back as Grace leaped into Connor's arms and the reunited brother and sister hugged one another.

Lorcan glanced away. The light was starting to lift in earnest now and he'd have to go inside. But although the light was coming, they were losing visibility as a mist had started to rise. But wasn't that a ship next to theirs? It was! How else could the boy have made it onto theirs? And now, as he looked through the deepening mist and the gathering light, Lorcan saw hordes of men standing alert on the opposite deck, armed with swords.

He looked back at Grace, who was still holding tight to her brother. This couldn't be a trick, could it? Was the other ship about to attack theirs?

Just then, a door opened and Darcy Flotsam stumbled out onto the deck.

Glancing up at the sky, she ran toward the bell. Without losing another precious moment, she began to toll it. As she did so, she noticed Grace and Lorcan and . . . a stranger. What was going on? Why was Lorcan here at this time? Who was the stranger? If only she hadn't overslept.

"Lorcan," cried Miss Flotsam, "go inside. It's dawn."

As the bell began to sound, Connor pulled back from Grace.

"What's happening?" he said.

"It's okay," Grace said. "It's called the Dawning Bell."

Back on *The Diablo,* Connor's friends struggled to see through the mist how things were going on the other deck.

As the bell started to sound, Bart gripped Cate's shoulder. "What's that?"

"I don't know, Bart. Some sort of alarm?"

"Connor needs our help," Bart said, grabbing his broad-sword.

"You don't know that," Cate said.

"I'm not waiting here to find out," Bart cried. Without another word, he ran across the wish, blinded momentarily by the settling mist.

He felt the deckboards under his feet and broke through the mist, seeing figures up ahead.

There was Connor, and a girl. That must be his sister. He could see the resemblance. Connor smiled. But there was another lad and a girl, too. And, as he ran up toward them, the lad darted forward and drew a cutlass.

Bart lifted his broadsword and swung it up to meet the face of the cutlass.

"No," cried Grace, confused by the attack. "Connor, stop him, stop him! Lorcan hasn't done me any harm."

"Lorcan, go inside!" cried Miss Flotsam.

But Lorcan ignored her, his attention focused only on the sword of his attacker. There *had* been some trick. Whoever had brought Grace's brother to the ship had come prepared to do battle with the Vampirates.

The light was starting to hurt his eyes now, but he was a good swordsman and he managed to land a direct hit on his attacker's arm.

Bart jumped backward. He wasn't used to being in the direct line of attack. Usually he encountered only fellow broadsworders, not vicious rapier bearers.

Connor pushed Grace aside and leaped in front of Bart, waving his rapier in Lorcan's face.

"Connor!" Grace cried. "No! Lorcan's my friend!"

"And Bart's mine," Connor cried, not daring to check over his shoulder to see if Bart was okay.

"Lorcan!" cried Miss Flotsam. "You *must* go inside. I need to take my position."

"Take it, Darcy," he cried. "Take your position and leave me be. I said I'd protect Grace and that's what I mean to do."

Sobbing, Miss Flotsam raced across the deck and jumped into her position as figurehead. Grace watched her quickly transform from living flesh to painted figurine.

Connor saw it, too, unable to believe his eyes.

"Lorcan, please go inside." Now it was Grace's turn to plead. Light was streaming onto the deck now and she could see the effect it was having on him. His eyes were closed and he was lashing out with his rapier to little effect.

"There's a ship of them, Grace," he cried, weak of breath. "They sent your brother to get you, but there's a horde waiting to follow. Like this one."

He pointed his sword at Bart.

"That isn't true," Connor said, "it's just me. They brought me here to get Grace, but that's all I want. I don't want to harm you."

"What about him?" Lorcan said, indicating Bart.

"I came when I heard the bell," Bart said. "I thought Connor was in danger. I thought you'd raised the alarm."

"That isn't an alarm," Grace said. "It's to clear the deck, not to fill it."

"So you're okay?" Bart asked.

"Yes," Grace said, smiling but still anxious to see Lorcan get safely inside.

"And you're not sending over any others?" Lorcan asked Bart.

"No, buddy, no way. I'm just here for my friend."

"Go inside, Lorcan," Grace said. "Please go inside."

The light was shining directly on his face now. It made him flail about and almost drop his sword.

"How do I know this isn't a trick?" he said.

"It isn't," said Connor. "I'm just here for Grace."

"Please, Lorcan. I trusted you. Now you must trust me."

"All right, Grace, all right."

At last Lorcan staggered back inside her cabin, grabbing the door as he fell and letting the sword slip from his hand.

"Look, I'll go back and tell the others everything is cool," Bart said. "Okay?"

Connor nodded.

As his friend departed, Connor looked at his sister again.

"I've got so much to tell you," he said.

"So have I," said Grace.

"And I've got something for you." Connor lifted his hand under his shirt and removed the locket, holding it out to her.

— ·—

Lorcan knew that he should close the door, but he had already been exposed to so much light that a small chink couldn't do him any further harm.

He watched Grace and her brother through the thin crack of light. He should feel happy for her, he thought. Happy that after all the upset she had been through, she was reunited with her brother at long last. She seemed happy now, as she took the locket into her hands and then placed it around her neck.

It was painful for Lorcan to watch. He didn't want it to be so. More than anything, he wanted to feel joy in his heart for Grace. And yet, as she snapped the locket into place around her neck, Lorcan felt the sadness of loss such as he had not felt in a long, long time.

His eyes were burning. At first he thought it was tears and he wiped them with his hand. But his eyes were dry, though they still burned.

Grace was safe. That was all that mattered. He'd sworn to protect her and his work was complete. He just needed to rest.

He stole one final glance at them but it was growing harder and harder to see them clearly. The mist was so thick on deck now that it created a veil between him and the twins. But it was more than that, he realized, as he finally closed the cabin door. He could not see properly even inside the cabin. The light seemed to have permanently damaged his eyes.

—⁓—

The strange mist completely encircled Grace and Connor now, until all they could see was each other. She still couldn't believe he was here. It was as if it had all been a dream. Well, a mixture of a nightmare and a dream.

"I missed you," she said.

"Missed you, too."

"And I miss Dad."

"Me too."

He opened his arms and hugged her tightly. Just for a moment it felt like they were back in the lighthouse with their dad. All safe.

How had he found her? And what would they do next? Would he join her on the Vampirate ship or would she follow him onto his? Was it time, after all, to return to Crescent Moon Bay?

But for now none of this mattered, she thought, dismissing the noisy questions. She hugged him tight. And as she did so, she realized that she'd been right all along. Now she knew what home meant. Now she not only knew it but felt it, too.

And as Grace hugged Connor and Connor hugged Grace and the mist circled around them, she heard the captain's whisper inside her head.

"So it ends. So it begins."

I'll tell you a tale of Vampirates,

A tale as old as true.

Yea, I'll sing you a song of an ancient ship,

And its mighty fearsome crew.

Yea, I'll sing you a song of an ancient ship,

That sails the oceans blue...

That haunts the oceans blue.

The Vampirate ship has tattered sails,

That flap like wings in flight.

They say that the captain, he wears a veil

So as to curtail your fright

At his death-pale skin

And his lifeless eyes

And his teeth as sharp as night.

Oh, they say that the captain, he wears a veil

And his eyes never see the light.